# THE MERCER BOYS IN THE GHOST PATROL

# THE MERCER BOYS IN THE GHOST PATROL

## CAPWELL WYCKOFF

**WILDSIDE PRESS**

Published by Wildside Press LLC.

www.wildsidebooks.com

# CHAPTER 1

## TERRY COMES TO GRIEF

A number of young men in the gray uniforms which formed the ordinary dress of the cadets at Woodcrest Military Institute stood around the counter in the school supply room. It was early in July and the summer encampment was at hand. It was the custom at Woodcrest for the third and second classmen to go to summer camp, while the younger classmen and the seniors went home for their vacation. The score or more of young soldiers who were in the supply room this July afternoon were busy getting their camping uniforms.

During the school year the neat, distinguished gray uniforms were worn, but on the encampment the more serviceable campaign uniforms, patterned after those worn by the United States Army, were required.

A tall, red-headed cadet, with twinkling eyes and a humorous expression perpetually on his good-natured, freckled face, was at the moment the next one to be waited on. He gave the sizes of his garments and then grinned.

"If it is convenient, I'd like a uniform in a shade to match my hair!" he requested. This grin was answered by half a dozen others, for Terry Mackson was a great favorite with his classmates in the new second class, into which he and his pals, the Mercer boys, had just graduated.

"We have nothing as red as all that," the cadet clerk grinned in return. "Would something in deep orange do?"

"Possibly it would, if you are careful to get something that won't conflict with my beauty!" returned the cadet.

"We haven't a thing in stock that would conflict with or detract from your beauty," said the clerk, gravely. "These uniforms are ugly in the extreme, and I'm sure you won't find them a drawback in the least, Mr. Mackson!"

"Well spoken, my lad!" said Terry. "Let's have the plainest uniform you have. Natural beauty ennobles whatever enshrines it, so bring out whatever you have!"

"Why bother with a uniform at all?" The cadet clerk laughed. "The colonel and the rest of us will be so busy admiring your looks that we won't notice anything else!"

There was a general laugh at this, as Dick Rowen, the cadet in charge of the commissary department, stepped to the counter, a frown on his face.

Rowen was a handsome young man with glossy black hair. He had never been popular with the cadet body, however, for he continually reminded everyone of the wealth and prestige of his family. But he was a very capable cadet and was respected though not popular. He had been placed in charge of the commissary department much to his annoyance, for he considered it beneath him. Rowen was striving for an officer's commission, and it did not please him to be "dud chucker," as the cadets called the commissary clerks. All day the endless routine of passing out uniforms, blouses, hats and shoes had galled him, and at the present moment his temper was ragged.

"What is the trouble here?" Cadet Rowen demanded crisply.

The clerk who was waiting on Terry turned to stare at him. "There's no trouble, Rowen," he said.

Rowen looked across the counter at Terry. "Is there any trouble, Mr. Mackson?"

Terry shook his head gravely. "No, Mr. Rowen. I am simply trying to draw a uniform that will match my beauty, that's all!"

Rowen frowned more deeply. "Have the goodness to understand, Mr. Mackson, that we are very busy here, and that such infant's prattle merely wastes our time!"

"All right, Papa!" said Terry sedately. The others snickered and Rowen grew angry.

"Please don't be funny, Mackson! That comes natural to some people, and others work hard all their lives without ever managing to be really humorous!"

Terry turned to the others back of him. "Gentlemen," he observed, "Mr. Rowen has turned philosopher! Some of you fellows are naturally funny, ask Mr. Rowen!"

A dull red flush mounted in the other's cheeks. "How long are you going to waste our time?"

"Look here!" exclaimed the redhead. "If I'm not mistaken, you are wasting your own time! Here I am, waiting with the patience of an angel for my uniform, and are you getting it? No, twenty times no! Don't you know that time wasted can never be recovered, Mr. Rowen?"

"I'll tell you what I do know!" Rowen fairly hissed. "I know that you and those Mercer brothers are too confounded stuck on yourselves! You are the colonel's own particular pets!"

"Well, well, the Mercer brothers get a tongue lashing, too!" said a brown-haired, good-looking youth back of Terry. "Brother Don, weep on my shoulder!"

"I cry better outdoors," grinned Don Mercer, behind his brother Jim. "Gee, how distressing this conversation is getting!"

"You are making us feel dreadful, really, Mr. Rowen!" Terry told the clerk mournfully. At the laugh that went up Rowen lost his temper.

"I'll make you feel dreadful, all right," snapped the disagreeable cadet, and before anyone could guess as to his purpose he hit Terry on the point of the jaw, knocking him to the floor.

There was a moment of hushed expectancy while Terry stared up at the supply clerk in surprise. Most of the good-natured grin had faded from his face, and a slight redness had suffused his cheeks. He jumped to his feet. But at that moment Colonel Morrell walked into the office.

Colonel Morrell was a little fat man with gray hair, laughing gray eyes and the air of a real man's man about him. By the cadet corps he was beloved greatly, and to a man they respected him thoroughly. His keen eye swept over the cadets and he noted that something unusual was in the wind, but with characteristic rare judgment he made no comment on it.

"Is everything going smoothly?" he asked the nearest clerk.

"Yes, sir," answered the cadet, saluting. The colonel returned the salute, turned on his heel and left the room. They heard his footsteps echo down the hall.

"Now, Mr. Rowen," murmured Terry. "This is what you need most of all!"

With that he seized the unprepared cadet by the collar, hauling him bodily over the counter. Rowen was unprepared for the act and flopped across the boards, his head hanging over the side. Although he struggled furiously Terry managed to hold him down while he administered a sound spanking to the surly one. Then he pushed him backward. The assembled cadets had enjoyed every moment of it.

"That's for you," said Terry, unheeding the sputtering of the other. "If you act like a baby someone will have to play papa and spank you! I happened to be the nearest one. Next time be careful who you punch on the jaw. It might be somebody who'll lose his temper and muss you up!"

"You—you red-headed calf!" cried the enraged Rowen. "I've—I've half a mind to thrash you!"

"Well, if you have half a mind, that means that your whole mind is busy on the one subject, because sometimes I think you have only half a mind. Now, you're wasting my time! One uniform, if you please!"

With very bad grace the uniform was handed to him and the line moved on. As Terry stepped away Rowen spoke to him between half-shut teeth. "I'll fix you for this yet, Mackson!"

Jim Mercer halted at the counter. "Was there some complaint about the Mercer brothers, Rowen?" he asked quietly.

"I just said that you two were the colonel's pets," replied the clerk. "Just because you two once helped the colonel out of a mess he bows down before you."

"With all due respect to the colonel," drawled Don Mercer, "he is a little too fat to bow down! Calm down, Dick."

"Aw, you guys give me a pain!" roared the clerk.

Terry impishly picked up the telephone, carefully holding down the hook. "Hello, is this the nurse?" He spoke into the transmitter. "If you have time I wish you'd stop in at the commissary department. Mr. Rowen has a very bad pain. I beg your pardon? Oh, it seems to be a Mackson-Mercer pain, if you know what that is! It seems to be—"

Laughing, Jim Mercer caught him by the arm. "Come on, get out of here, you!" he admonished his friend. "Come on up to the room."

The three boys were devoted pals, having been friends from childhood. They had been in many scrapes and adventures together, sharing their fun and dangers on land and sea. In the first volume of this series, *The Mercer Boys' Cruise in the Lassie*, they had gone on a long cruise, and from there they had come to Woodcrest, their fun and adventure at that time being related in *The Mercer Boys at Woodcrest*. On their following summer vacation they had encountered some strange events in *The Mercer Boys on a Treasure Hunt* and later on had worked together on a school mystery, details of which will be found in *The Mercer Boys' Mystery Case*. Early in the spring of that same year the boys had faced a man's task on the Massachusetts coast, all of which will be found in the fifth volume, *The Mercer Boys with the Coast Guard*. Now, after a few months of uneventful school life, they were preparing for their first encampment.

Once in their own room the three boys hung up the new uniforms that they would wear the next day. There were no lessons and they had nothing to do except wait until morning, when they would set off for camp. All of the boys looked forward eagerly to it.

"I hear that we are going to a new camping ground this year," Jim said, as he sat on the edge of his bed. "Rustling Ridge, they call it."

"Yes," nodded Don. "Other years they have held the encampment at Perryville, but the colonel hunted up new grounds this time. I heard that there had been quite a bit of building going on near the old camp and the colonel wants to get as far away from civilization as he can."

"Rustling Ridge is none too far, at that," observed Terry.

"No, it isn't," agreed Jim. "But it is far enough away for camping purposes. Even the colonel doesn't know much about this new location."

"About thirty miles from here, isn't it?" Don asked.

"I heard that it was," returned Terry. "Well, the whole outlook suits me perfectly. I wouldn't have known what to do with myself this vacation, anyway."

"We might have made a cruise," Don suggested. "We haven't been sailing on the good old Lassie for so long that I'm afraid I've forgotten how to manage it!"

"Camping might bring us some good adventures," Jim put in. Don shrugged his shoulders.

"I rather doubt that. What adventures can we run across on a camping trip? We'll have a lot of fun, I grant you that, but I don't look for anything out of the way. We'll be very busy drilling and practicing all sorts of tactics."

"We might have some excitement with Mr. Rowen!" Terry grinned.

"Rowen is a natural sorehead," said Don briefly. "The best thing we can do is to let him alone. That kind isn't made any better by stirring up, and he isn't worth getting into trouble over. We can just be decent to him and let it go at that."

"I guess you're right," nodded Terry.

Supper that night was a slightly unruly affair, tempered only by the presence of the colonel and the other officers. The young soldiers themselves were in high spirits.

Rowen, after the meal, went into conference with his two roommates, young men who had borrowed from the unpopular cadet and, therefore, felt obligated to him. What went on in that conference was not designed for Terry Mackson's peace.

When the orders of the day were read that evening all cadets were commanded to be in place at bugle call in the morning, with full equipment and ready to march. It was announced that no excuses would be accepted for failure to report on time.

When the bugle sounded the next morning the cadets sprang from bed, dressed and ate a hearty breakfast. There was still half an hour before assembly and the cadets were at leisure. Just as Terry was turning away from the table a member of the kitchen force approached him. In his hand he had a note.

"This is for you, Mr. Mackson," he said. "Thanks, Pete," said Terry, accepting the note. "Who gave it to you?"

"Jack Olson," replied the cook. "He said Captain Rush gave it to him, but he didn't have time to give it to you himself."

Terry nodded and read the note. Captain Rush was the leader of the artillery division to which Terry belonged. The note was brief and to the point.

Mr. Mackson:
> Go to the storage room in the barn and get out the extra harness that you will find there.

Rush, Captain.

"Funny he didn't tell me, instead of sending me a note," reflected Terry. "Well, orders are orders, and I'm ready as it is. I'll go out there now."

He made his way to the barn, finding it quite empty. He knew that there was a small storage room at one side and he made his way to it, opening the door and peering in. There was a pile of harness on the floor and he went toward it.

At that moment the door back of him closed with a bang. A bolt on the outside was shot at the same moment. Terry rushed to the door, pushing against it.

"Hey!" he shouted. "Open this door, whoever you are!"

His only answer was the sound of retreating footsteps and the point of it all came to him in a rush. He kicked against the door, finding it solid and then looked around the cell. But there was no window and no opening of any kind.

"Tumbled right into the trap!" he groaned, grinding his teeth. "If I don't get out of here before assembly it will be too bad for me!"

# CHAPTER 2

## THE "GOSSIP" RUNS WILD

The whole trick was clear to him now. In the general orders of the day, read to the cadets on the previous day, the fact that no excuse would be accepted had been sternly emphasized. Terry was not the kind who would carry tales even if he thought they would excuse him and win him sympathy, and as he realized how badly fooled he had been his eyes flashed in anger.

"I see the whole business, now/' he reflected. "Jack Olson is a crony of Rowen's and he carried that note supposedly signed by Rush. They know I won't tell Rush about it, and there isn't any use in thumping Olson, because he probably had to take his orders from Rowen. But I sure would like my hands on that surly guy!"

Realizing that every moment counted the redheaded youth looked around the small room, his eyes having grown used to the darkness. He hoped that there might be some instrument that would make it possible for him to pry up a board and so make his escape, but the only thing in sight was the pile of harness. There was not even a piece of metal on the harness and although he examined every corner of the little cell he was unable to find a single object that would aid him.

"Guess I'll just have to use my hands and feet, if that will do any good," he reflected.

Dropping on his hands and knees he examined the floor carefully to see if any of the boards were loose, but all of them were securely fastened to the huge beams that made up the framework of the barn. The boards were very thick and any thought of escaping under the barn was out of the question. From there he went to the door, feeling carefully along the sides to see if any signs of weakness existed here, but once again he was disappointed. Like the rest of the barn the door and the frame had been strongly constructed and it did not even quiver under his hearty kicks.

"About the only thing I can do—if I can do it—is to kick a board off the side of the wall," he decided.

With this thought in mind he raised his foot, but then a sound reached his ears, a sound that made his blood chill.

With a clarity and snap the call of assembly rang out on the morning air!

"Good night!" groaned Terry, the sweat breaking out on his forehead. "There goes the call to assemble! If I'm ever going to get out of here in time, now is the moment!"

With desperation Terry kicked stoutly at the wall boards, but with the first kick the bitter truth was forced upon him. The sides of the barn were as strongly composed as the rest of the building, and all the kicking in the world would not get him out of the room in which he was held prisoner. To further worry him certain sounds told him that the process of assembly was going forward rapidly.

Doors slammed, running footsteps sounded on the parade grounds, voices rang out as the assembling cadets gathered. The butt of a rifle cracked on the pavement, and the noise of stamping horses reached his ears. The cavalrymen, of which Jim Mercer was the chief, were leading out the spirited mounts, and the creaking of leather, the snorts of the horses, and the cries of the young soldiers, reached the ears of the unfortunate young cadet. Hoping to attract their attention he pounded and yelled at the top of his voice, but no response came back to him. They were making too much noise themselves to hear him.

Closer at hand there was a deeper rumble and Terry groaned in spirit. It was the members of his own division, the artillery, taking out the field guns that they were to take with them for the summer practice. He was the chief gunner on the sleek steel monster which he had named the "Gossip" and he knew that the others of his crew must be wondering where he was. Just as soon as the guns were in formation and the roll call sounded he would be officially marked absent from duty and held guilty of disobeying orders. As he heard the guns roll out of the barracks and heard the noise of the towing cables being connected he knew it was too late.

From the barracks to the parade ground there was a slight hill and the trucks began to pull the weapons up the grade. He heard them go up one by one and then something seemed to go wrong. There was a snap, a rumble and somebody cried out.

"Look out!" he heard Captain Rush bellow. "Number One gun is loose!"

That gun was Terry's own piece of equipment.

From the cries that arose he gathered that the gun had broken from the cable and was rolling down the hill. There was an increasing rumble that seemed suddenly close at hand, and before his brain had time to realize what had happened there was a tremendous crash, the boards of his cell burst open like matchwood, and the butt of the "Gossip" halted a scant foot from his stomach!

For a single instant Terry was stunned. The sudden glare of morning sunlight made him blink, the dust filled his mouth and the echoes of the crash remained in his ears. But it did not take him long to regain his composure and spring forward. He placed affectionate hands on the gun.

"Good old 'Gossip,'" he whooped. "You wouldn't go on parade without me, would you? Talk about luck!"

A half dozen artillerymen appeared at the opening, led by Captain Rush. At the sight of Terry they halted and stared in amazement.

"Where have you been?" Cadet Emerson, Terry's mate, shouted.

"Waiting for the old 'Gossip' to let me out!" retorted Terry gleefully.

Rush approached him. "Where have you been, Mr. Mackson?" he inquired formally.

"Someone locked me in here and I couldn't get out, captain," returned Terry.

"Then the accident was a lucky one for you," nodded the captain. He turned to the young artillerymen. "We have only a few minutes to make the parade grounds. Snap to it!"

Terry threw himself into the work, rejoicing in the chance to be busy. The truck was backed down the hill and the broken cable was stripped from it and new material substituted. A loose pin was driven into the shaft and when the "Gossip" was harnessed it was drawn up to the top of the hill in safety and wheeled swiftly into position. And on the rear box sat Terry, grinning from ear to ear.

When his name was called he answered brightly, stealing a look across the parade ground to the infantry, where Rowen stood in the second rank. The face of the sullen one was a study in amazement.

In accordance with previous instructions the cavalry swung out first, taking the long, dusty road that led to Rustling Ridge. Next in line marched the infantry and the artillery rumbled in the rear. Terry sat on his gun, happy and thankful for the good fortune he had had. He smiled frequently, but there was a grim set to his jaw nevertheless.

All through the morning they marched and it was noon before they paused to make temporary camp. Just as soon as the long column came to a halt and broke up Terry made his way to where Rowen and his few friends sat on a grassy bank. He halted directly in front of the other.

"Didn't work, did it?" Terry asked.

Rowen looked at him with a haughty frown. "I don't know what you are talking about," he said.

"Yes, you do. Your plan to lock me in the barn until I was late for camp didn't turn out very well, did it?"

"I don't know anything about it, and you can't prove that I do," snapped the dark-haired boy.

"Don't be silly!" growled Terry. "I can do that easily. All I have to do is to give that little sneak Jack Olson a good, stiff beating and he'll tell. Look at how pale he is! Or I can ask Captain Rush about it and we'd have you in a fine mess. But I don't intend to do anything like that, Rowen, and you know it. I would have been blacklisted by my captain if I had been late for encampment, and you figured on that. Now, look here! Just one more piece of freshness out of you and I'll give you the peachiest licking you ever saw, right in front of the cadet corps. Don't forget it, my friend!"

Turning on his heel Terry walked off, his eyes dancing slightly. There was no word spoken by the ones back of him, and perhaps it was just as well. The redhead was dynamite and ready to go.

In that brief period he encountered Don. Jim was far ahead with the supply corps but Don, who was a lieutenant in the infantry, was close at hand. He was delighted to see his pal.

"Where in the world were you at assembly?" Don demanded. "Jim and I nearly turned the building upside down looking for you."

Terry explained briefly and Don approved of his recent charge to Rowen. "That fellow certainly has a grudge against you," said Don. "You couldn't exactly call him a bully, because he isn't big enough or strong enough, but his surly nature makes him anything but trustworthy. A fine mess you would have had if you had been several days late for encampment. As far as that goes, you might have been a prisoner in that storage room for a long time."

"That's right," agreed Terry. "And to anyone who likes to eat as well as I do that would have meant something!"

After an afternoon of leisurely marching the cadets came to an open meadow where the cavalry and the supply corps had set up tents. Here they spent the night and the next morning they pushed on to Rustling Ridge, arriving there about noontime.

Rustling Ridge was a long slope that rose gradually from a flat meadow. It was in the heart of delightful country, and here and there solitary farmhouses could be seen. Close beside the camp there was a deep swimming hole, which the cadets welcomed with unrestrained delight. The camp itself was pitched in a grove about a quarter way up the slope, the white tents rising in somewhat irregular lines between the trees. The wide glades on either side of the camp permitted the creation of natural centers for the horses and the supply wagons and guns. By mid afternoon the camp was in first-class order and the tired cadets enjoyed their first swim in the near-by swimming hole.

After supper large fires were lighted, but the cadets did not linger long around them. Even before taps many of them had sought their cots, falling asleep as soon as they crawled in between their blankets. Sentries were posted and soon the camp was quiet except for the stamping of horses and the tramp of the sentries.

# CHAPTER 3

## AT RUSTLING RIDGE

The clear, thrilling strains of the bugle made scores of cadets cordially hate Bugler Howes on the following morning. Many a young soldier considered defying orders and sleeping on in peace and comfort, but wisdom prevailed in the long run. With a snap and many groans the camp came to life.

"Oh, boy!" sighed Terry, casting his blankets to one side. "I never felt less like getting up in all my life!"

"I don't see why you or Jim should kick," Don said, as he pulled on his clothes. "You two rode out here but I had to march all the way!"

"I'm tired just the same," said Terry.

Once awake the cadets came alive to the glories of camp life. A rush was made to the near-by brook where they washed, and then dressing was speedily finished. Before long they had fallen in for inspection, the reading of orders and the march to breakfast.

A long tent had been erected for meals in bad weather, but during the clear and warm weather they were permitted to eat outside around the kitchen tent.

Before long they were all hard at work. On a flat plain at the bottom of the hill they were all required to drill and take routine exercises during the morning. This took up their time until noon. Then, in the afternoon, the units took up the tactics of their own particular division. The infantry was busy that day with setting up range targets for practice in the near future. After that was over they worked steadily fixing the camp. Tents were made more inviting by the addition of wooden floors, pegs were put in with a view toward real strength and service, and trenches were dug to carry off the rain water when it fell from the sloping canvas. A permanent kitchen was constructed and the long tables for the mess tent were built and put in place. Benches then were hammered into place along the tables, the wagons set in proper formation and the camp looked vastly improved.

The cavalry escaped this task but was busy with tactics of its own. Under Jim, who was its chief, it was required to drill and go for a canter across the country. That used up most of the afternoon and the sun was beginning to sink when they returned. At school, during the term, the cavalrymen got quite a bit of practice, but it was the plan of the colonel to teach his boys to ride every day during the encampment, so that they might become used to having horses under them a good many hours at a stretch. Many a young man found himself stiff and sore before the end of the week.

The artillery was busy with what they called "silent drill." Artillery practice was always pretty expensive and only during the fall and the last few weeks of summer encampment did the colonel allow any firing of the fieldpieces. During the summer the artillerymen were instructed in the art of finding the range, wheeling the guns into position, effectively concealing them from an enemy, especially an enemy in the air, and tearing down and rebuilding the guns.

With all of these activities the first day in camp sped by with astonishing rapidity. This first day was different from the ones that followed, for once the camp was settled the work decreased materially. So busy had the boys been that there was no time for a swim or any fun on that initial day of camp life. A few hardy souls managed to stay awake and talk and sing songs around the campfires, but most of the young men stumbled to bed at the first possible moment.

The three friends had not had much of a chance to see each other that day, and at night they were too tired to do much in the way of talking. In common with many others they sought their beds before taps.

"If I'm going to be as tired as this every night I'll never enjoy this camping trip," Jim grumbled as he undressed.

"You won't be," Don observed. "This was an unusual day for all of us, but well get used to it. With all our outdoor life, this systematic drill, exercise, and work makes us feel the grind."

"I don't see why we have to take regular exercises." Terry yawned and stretched out on his cot. "Seems to me that we get enough to keep us physically fit as it is."

"Yes, but the kind of routine exercises that we get help to keep us limbered up," Don returned. "Otherwise, we'd get a whole lot of one kind of training and not much of another. You and I get plenty of leg and arm exercise but Jim would be riding all day if he stuck to his particular branch of the corps."

"That's true," agreed Terry. "Well, I suppose the colonel and the officers know what we need most of. If anybody asked me right now, though, I'd say it was sleep."

On the second day things came more easily to the active young soldiers. At first, stiff and sore muscles cried out in protest and glum faces characterized the corps. But as the day went on their hearts cheered and slowly the joy of camping evidenced itself.

That afternoon they finished drill and maneuvers at three o'clock and from then on the time was their own. A dozen games of baseball were quickly organized but most of the boys preferred to make a rush for the big swimming hole. Before many minutes a score of the boys splashed in.

One cadet had dropped in first to test the depth of the stream, and finding that it was up to the average boy's shoulder at the bank and about ten feet deep in the center, a number of boys had dived joyfully in. Don and Terry were among the first, with Jim following a little later.

"This is a dandy pool," gasped Jim, shaking the water from his eyes and floating close beside Don. "I like snappy fresh water even better than I do the salt water."

"I don't," returned his brother. "I like the rush and the sting of the green sea water. But this woodland water makes you work to keep afloat."

There was no springboard and the cadets were diving from the bank. In time this proved disappointing. As they clambered up the sides, the water running in streams from their dripping bathing trunks made the bank muddy and then dangerously slippery. More than one sloppy fall plastered a swimmer with mud and caused gleeful laughter, until a few cadets ran into camp, brought out some long boards and some thick supports, and in a very short time a fairly good diving board had been placed on the bank.

"This is some improvement," smiled Harry Douglas, as he tried the board out.

The diving then became general and was enjoyed. One of the best divers was Dick Rowen. His summers had been spent largely in summer resorts where swimming was the principal attraction and he had become quite expert at it. Knowing that the eyes of many of his comrades were upon him Rowen performed a good many fancy dives, all of which were very well done. Some of the cadets, with quiet generosity, complimented him upon his prowess.

"Oh, diving comes easily to me," answered Rowen, poising for another, in answer to a word of praise from a cadet. "This is one of my best."

He jumped to the springboard, attempted to turn around and over, but his twist did not work and his feet slipped. Truth to tell, the cadets were growing tired of his posing and a delighted shout went up as he slapped the water with a sound that echoed over the camp.

Thoroughly angry, Rowen bobbed up out of the water and scrambled ashore, turning a resentful ear to the good-natured teasing of his mates. Jim was the next one to follow Rowen out on the board, and he prepared for his dive.

"Going to give us an exhibition of your best dive, Jim?" Cadet Vench called out, laughing.

Jim grinned. "Yes, this is my best," he answered, and sprang away. But his foot slipped and he hit the water in the same way that Rowen had. Instantly a roar of laughter went up and Rowen's face flushed a dull red.

Jim made his way out of the water. "That wasn't so good at that," he remarked, as he gained the bank. Then he came face to face with Rowen.

"Think you're pretty smart, don't you, Mercer?" hissed the cadet.

Jim looked surprised. "Why, no, not especially. Not after that dive, anyway. What do you mean, Dick?"

"Don't call me Dick!" snapped Rowen. "I'm only Dick to my friends, and that doesn't include you. I said you think you're funny because you ridiculed me in that dive!"

"Oh, don't be silly!" said Jim. "I had no intention of imitating you, Rowen. My foot honestly slipped, that's all."

"I don't believe you, Mercer," said Rowen, at a white heat.

There was a moment's pause and the gathered cadets looked on with interest. Jim's jaw had set and he thought a moment before replying.

"Listen, Rowen," he said, when he had gained sufficient control of himself. "I want you to understand one thing. I only joke with a man who is,, enough of a man to take a joke. If I were picking out anyone to have some fun with I wouldn't pick a sorehead like you. As for my not being a friend of yours, Rowen, that is your own fault."

"Fault!" said Rowen, trembling. "Jeepers! Do you think I care that you aren't my friend?"

"Whatever you like." Jim nodded and turned away. Unheeding the statement that "some fellows made him sick" Jim went back into the water, to enjoy himself and forget Rowen.

That evening the cadets remained up until taps, which came at nine-thirty. A number of fires formed convenient places for them to gather and chat. Just before taps the three friends went to their tents.

"I didn't notice Rowen around tonight," remarked Don, as they began to prepare for bed.

"Might have been sulking in his tent," grinned Terry. "Now, the only thing that remains is for him to pick a fight with you, Don!"

"I don't know if I could be as patient as you two have been," mused Don. "I think I should be tempted to punch his nose for him!"

"Don't worry," smiled Jim, "we were tempted, all right!"

"Who took my bayonet?" asked Terry, suddenly.

All of the cadets, including the artillerymen and cavalrymen, were required to have guns and bayonets, and Terry had looked aimlessly at his equipment, to note that the bayonet was gone. In a moment Don reported the loss of his.

"Mine's gone, too," announced Jim. "This looks funny to me."

Terry threw the blankets off his bed. "Not under the covers," he murmured. "Now, where—hey!"

He dropped to his knees and looked under the cot. Then he reached under and brought out his weapon.

"Look under your cots," he directed. Don and Jim did so and uttered a sharp cry.

"Sticking upright, so that when we lay down on the bed the point would prod us," Don growled.

"And that explains where Rowen was this evening," guessed Terry.

"Say, this is going a little too far!" cried Jim. "That's a dangerous trick."

"Well, not especially dangerous," said Don slowly. "The point wasn't in such a position that it would have actually run into us. But he figured that we'd come in just at taps and jump into bed, landing on the points with enough force to make us squirm. The worst part of it all is that we can't prove who did it."

"From now on," said Terry, his eyes narrowing, "we have got to keep a wary eye on that guy."

"Yes," nodded Don. "I guess he placed all three bayonets so that one of the disliked boys would be sure to get it. It would be funny if it had been me, who so far has done nothing to antagonize him."

"If I catch him in any funny business I'll sail right into him," promised Jim, as they replaced the bayonets in the scabbards.

Taps rang out and the camp quieted down. In a moment the three boys drifted off to sleep.

# CHAPTER 4

## STRANGE TALES FROM THE RIDGE

Three shots sounded from the east side of the camp. Almost on top of them three shots sounded from a point close by.

With the first shots the three friends stirred and woke up, listening while half asleep. But with the second three shots they rose up in their beds, wide awake.

Close at hand the sound of rapidly turning wheels reached their ears, accompanied by the beat of horses' hoofs. Something metallic bumped and banged. A voice called out: "Corporal of the guard! Post Number Three!"

The boys jumped from their cots with one accord, reaching for their clothes.

"Something wrong with the sentries," cried Don.

"Who is at Number Three post?" asked Jim.

"Anderson," answered Terry, fumbling with his shoes.

The camp was in motion. Lights flashed at various points and voices sounded. Past the tent went running feet. But the bugle did not sound, so they knew that it was not a fire or any similar emergency.

"I'm ready. How about you two?" Don called.

"Right with you," was the response and the three soldiers burst out of the tent.

A central fire was burning and at this point the colonel was standing, half-clad and with mussed-up hair, his eyes heavy with sleep. The other cadets were clustering around him there, and the sentries were straggling in to that center.

Just as the three boys reached the spot the sentries from Number Three and Number Four posts came up and saluted.

Number Three post was at a point up the Ridge and Number Four was right at the edge of camp. The shots from Number Four had followed so closely to those from Number Three that they knew the same thing had caused both signals.

"Sentries to report, sir," announced the corporal of the guard, saluting.

The colonel saluted and faced the sentries. "Make your report, gentlemen," he ordered.

Anderson, from Number Three post spoke up. "While patrolling my post I heard a wagon coming along that dirt road just above the camp on the Ridge. It appeared to be coming at a great rate of speed and just as it reached a point above my post it left the road and cut right down through the bushes toward me. It had a man and a boy in it and I challenged them, but without slacking speed a single bit the wagon tore right past me toward the camp. I then fired the shots to warn the camp and the next sentry."

"Very good," nodded the colonel. "Mr. Simms?"

"I heard the shots, though I had heard the thrashing of the wagon previously," spoke up the second sentry. "I turned to find the wagon bearing down on me, swinging from side to side, and with a man and boy hanging onto the seat. It cut straight across the lower end of the camp grounds, down the slope and across the drill grounds. I fired to bear out Mr. Anderson."

"Very good, gentlemen," said the colonel, with a puzzled frown on his forehead. In the momentary silence that followed they could hear the mysterious wagon bumping and banging across the country, apparently at top speed.

Now that the official reports had been given the talk became general. The incident was extremely puzzling. Both sentries remarked that the man and boy had been huddled together much as though pretty badly frightened, and the sight of the cadets with guns had not seemed to reassure them any. Neither sentry had been able to see what had been in the wagon because it had passed them in too great a hurry, but from the sound they judged the rattling was caused by pots and pans. A single horse had pulled the cart.

"Strangest thing I ever heard of," murmured the new senior captain, Henry Jordan.

"I can't figure out why the party in the wagon left the dirt road," said the colonel to Major Rhodes, the drill instructor. "That road runs parallel with the Ridge and works gradually down to the level of the countryside. For some reason or other that pair in the wagon wanted to get off the Ridge and out on the open meadow."

"It is possible that they were fleeing from some crime," suggested Rhodes.

"True enough," assented the colonel. "And when they saw the cadets the vision didn't reassure them any. Well, it goes beyond my understanding." He turned once more to the attentive soldiers. "Corporal of the guard, restation the sentries. Everyone back to his bed."

The sentries were reposted and the other cadets straggled back to their cots. Once in their tent Jim looked at his watch.

"A quarter past three," he announced. "Quite an uncanny hour out here in the country. I'll bet there is something behind that wild wagon flight."

"Funny they should cut right across the camp," remarked Don.

"I agree with Rhodes that those fellows were probably fleeing from something like a crime," advanced Terry.

"That may be the explanation," agreed Don. "I can't think of any other reason for such a wild flight. Well, me for some more sleep."

The rest of that night was quiet and in the morning the cadets discussed the event further. The details of the day then took up all of their attention and the night adventure was pushed from their minds.

Late in the afternoon Don and Terry hastened into the tent to get their baseball gloves. Jim was in the tent at the time.

"Going to play some ball?" Terry hailed.

Jim shook his head. "I'm out of luck today," he announced. "Six of us have to go to a near-by farmhouse and buy some eggs and butter. The colonel told me to try and strike a bargain with a farmer for eggs, butter, milk and meat."

"Don't forget to wait for your change after you pay the farmer!" advised Terry.

"Go chase yourself!" flung back Jim. "I guess I know enough for that."

While the other two went off to play ball Jim rounded up his five companions and they set off on horseback for the farmhouses that lay scattered over the Ridge. Two of the farms they passed did not look very promising but at last they came to a neat-looking one which had a large sign on the front fence. This sign announced that chickens, eggs and butter were on sale and into this yard the six cavalrymen turned their horses. An uproar of barking dogs announced their presence and a farmer appeared, scanning their uniforms with great interest. To him Jim explained their errand.

The farmer was more than pleased and hastened to bring out several dozen fresh eggs and a dozen pounds of butter. In the meantime some children and two farmhands had gathered about the soldiers, staring at them curiously. When the supplies had been paid for Jim asked the farmer to come to camp and confer with the colonel concerning future food supplies. The farmer was delighted beyond words.

"You bet your boots I'll come down," he cried. "Business is mighty poor, and this is a big boost to me. My name's Carson."

A little boy named Jimmie was particularly interested in the cadets, and they took an instant liking to him. He was a bright and sturdy little boy, and some of the cadets invited him to visit the camp, an invitation which he willingly accepted.

Just before they rode off the farmer spoke to Jim. "Ain't see nothing of the ghost, have you?" he asked.

Jim shook his head. "No. Have you one?"

The farmer nodded solemnly. "Haven't you heard about the ghost of Rustling Ridge?" he asked.

"No, we haven't," laughed Lieutenant Thompson.

"There is a sure-enough ghost that prowls this Ridge," said the farmer, gravely. "Every once in a while it walks and scares people half to death. More than one family's up and moved away just on account of him."

"So far we haven't been lucky enough to see him," returned Jim, distributing the packages. "If we do, we'll try and take him apart and look at him."

The farmer shook his head. "Very bad business, that ghost. Look out he doesn't turn up in your camp some night."

With more jests about the ghost the cadets swung out of the yard and headed back toward camp, carrying their packages carefully.

"So there is a ghost on the Ridge, is there?" Thompson said to Jim.

"I'm not greatly surprised," Jim said. "Most of these country places have room for at least one good ghost. They wouldn't be quite happy if they didn't."

The colonel was pleased at their success and planned to buy more things from the farmer in the future. The provisions, with the exception of the canned goods which they had brought with them from school, had been all used up, for the invigorating outdoor life gave all the cadets ravenous appetites.

The cadets had been asleep perhaps two hours that night when a medley of shots rang out from post Number One, deep in the woods. As on the previous night the three boys hopped out of bed immediately.

"Golly, this is getting to be an epidemic," snorted Terry.

"But this must be something different," remarked Don. "I don't hear any wagon crashing through the bushes."

"There aren't any more shots, either," mentioned Jim.

Once outside the corporal of the guard brought in Douglas from the post. The colonel asked for a report.

"While standing at my post I saw a white shape pass me about ten yards away!" was Harry's startling statement. "I challenged it, but it just glided on past me. At my shots it flashed into the trees and was gone. I was unable to find any trace of it."

"A shape, Mr. Douglas?" frowned the colonel. "What sort of a shape?"

"Well, it looked like someone in a sheet," explained Douglas. "I couldn't see any head on the object, and it seemed to glide along the ground!"

"Hmm, our ghost of the Ridge!" said Jim to Thompson.

"What was that, Mr. Mercer?" the colonel cried, alertly.

Jim explained the story which the farmer had told to them that afternoon. "We didn't say anything about it, because we put it down for a lot of nonsense," he wound up.

"I see," replied the colonel. "Captains and lieutenants go to post Number One and look around."

The others waited a long half-hour until the officers came back. There was no news.

"We found no traces of anything," Senior Captain Jordan reported.

Puzzled over the events of the past two nights the colonel ordered the boys back to bed. It was a long time before a good many of them fell asleep. In their own tent the three pals talked quietly of the situation, but could not puzzle it out.

"If this business doesn't stop pretty soon," Terry concluded the talk, "we won't get enough sleep on this camping trip!"

# CHAPTER 5

## A FIGHT AND A STAMPEDE

CAPTAIN JIM made his way around the last of the tents that formed the A Company row and then paused. With a motion that combined speed with caution he stepped out of sight behind the slope of the tent, his eyes narrowed, senses alert.

He was on his way to the section of the camp allotted to the cavalry horses. It was mid afternoon and active drill was over for the day. Most of the young soldiers were in swimming, a few played baseball out in the blazing sun, and a few with less energy lay in the shade. Jim had dismounted rather hurriedly to make a report and he was on his way to see that the cadet orderlies had properly taken care of his horse.

The horses were just before him at the present moment, a score or more of restless, high-strung mounts. No orderly or cavalryman was with them at the moment and no one save one cadet could be seen. This cadet was acting queerly, and Jim's attention was the more quickly attracted when he saw that the lone cadet was Dick Rowen.

Rowen's campaign hat was in his crooked arm and he was standing directly in front of Jim's horse, Squall. From time to time Rowen looked furtively around the camp to see if anyone was observing him, but he failed to see the cavalry captain. The lone cadet dipped his hand into the hat and extended something to the horse. Squall appeared to reach out eagerly for whatever it was each time, but the neck of another horse obscured from Jim what it was that Rowen was feeding his horse.

"Now, what the dickens can that fellow be doing?" Jim puzzled. "He seems to be unusually kind to my horse, and it looks suspicious to me. Of course, it is possible that Rowen likes horses and is feeding them, but he knows that one is mine. Maybe he doesn't carry his grudges as far as the animals!"

One of the objects that Rowen was feeding to the horse dropped to the ground, rolling a short distance. As soon as Jim recognized it he became indignant.

"A green apple! A lot he knows about horses! If he wants to be kind to them he should pick something else beside—"

He stopped short in his thought. Rowen looked right and left again and then moved off a few paces to the left, reaching down for a bucket of water. With this in his hand he walked back to the horse, raised it to his eager lips, and tilted the bucket.

Jim Mercer waited to see no more. The whole cowardly trick was plain to him now. Each cavalryman was required to keep his mount in perfect condition and no excuse would be accepted for failure to do so. He could picture Squall after his meal of green apples and his drink of cold water, rolling in agony for hours, and himself severely blamed for criminal neglect. The boy's eyes blazed in fury as he hurled himself in Rowen's direction.

He was on top of the boy before Rowen was aware of him. Rowen turned startled eyes in his direction, his face paling swiftly. The tongue of the horse had just touched the water's surface when Jim landed his fist with all his force on the cheek of the cadet.

Rowen went down promptly, the bucket of water spilling all over his uniform. A dull red spot showed where Jim's fist landed, and Rowen rolled over with a faint bleat. With bulging eyes he looked up to where Jim towered over him.

"Why, you contemptible, sneaking coward!" Jim, his voice trembling, exploded with emotion. "You intended to bloat my horse so that I would do 'growl duty' for neglect, did you? How about the hours of agony that the horse would suffer? Did you think of that? Get on your feet, because I'm going to thrash you until you won't be able to walk for the rest of the summer!"

"If you lay your hands on me, Mercer, I'll report you to the colonel," cried Rowen, cowed at Jim's attitude. The captain was ablaze with wrath.

"Tell the colonel all you want to, but I'm going to put you in the infirmary for a month," promised Jim, reaching for the collar of the fallen cadet.

At that moment Terry, Jordan, Don and Vench came around the end of the tent row. They had been playing ball and were on their way to change clothes for a swim. They saw the two before them and hurried over.

"Look here, gentlemen," commanded Jordan, briskly. "You can't fight in camp. What's the row, anyway?"

"Mercer knocked me down," complained Rowen, while Don pulled Jim away. Don was surprised to feel how violently Jim was trembling.

"Why did you knock Rowen down, Mercer?" Jordan asked.

Jim did not in the least mind Jordan's commanding tone. Although they were both captains of divisions, and Jim was therefore an equal as an officer, Jordan nevertheless claimed a slight privilege as the senior captain of the school. In the following year, their last one at Woodcrest, Jim would be senior captain of the cavalry, with the unusual record of having held that post for three years. His heroism at Hill 31, when he rescued Vench, had won him that rank. But in the final year Don would be promoted from the infantry lieutenant to Senior Cadet Captain of the Corps, thus ranking a step higher than Jim, for all the latter's three years of captaincy in the cavalry.

Jim readily related the story of the short fight. He felt that the action was so cowardly and sneaking that Rowen did not deserve to have it hushed up. The faces of the cadets described their feelings as the story was told. Rowen turned white then red-faced as he saw the looks cast in his direction.

"I don't care so much about the punishment I would have received," Jim said in conclusion, "but how any guy in the world with a grain of common decency in him would stoop to give a horse hours of agony is more than I can see. You fellows can see the evidences of his guilt on the ground, the pail and the apple. When you came along I was about to give him the biggest licking he ever got in his life!"

"Get up, Rowen!" commanded the senior captain, sternly. "We are not on duty, or I'd put up with this trick just long enough to order you under arrest! I don't mind telling you frankly that you won't last long enough in the corps to ever graduate if this story gets out!"

"I don't care a hang about the corps!" said Rowen. "How about Mercer here? Don't forget that he struck me."

"I won't forget him for doing it, instead I will remember him gratefully for doing it. Perhaps it was too bad that we arrived just as we did." Rowen looked up at Jordan shamefaced yet still belligerent. "I'll get even with you boys! Just wait and see. And you can't prove I harmed your old horse, either, Mercer." With these remarks, Rowen turned on his heel and strode away, his chin high in the air.

"Gee! How do you like that?" Terry exclaimed. "He sure has some nerve carrying a grudge after what's happened just now!"

"I thought I had met up with a lot of the mean, tricky people!" exclaimed Jordan. "But that beats me!"

"What about the horse, Jim?" Don asked.

"I'll have to duck over to the canteen and get out some of the horse medicine and then run him around until he gets over the effects of the green apples," replied the cavalry captain. "No water for you, Squall old boy, until you have lost the effects of your unexpected meal."

While Jim was looking after the horse the others walked over to the tents, talking the matter over. All of them were deeply upset by the total unjustness of it all.

"Just because Jim slipped on the springboard and made a dive like Rowen's!" said Vench. "I can't understand some fellows."

"Well, I'll tell you," replied Don, slowly. "For a long time Rowen has had a grouch against all of us, for no particular reason at all. He's the kind of boy who just seems to have trouble wherever he goes."

It was not until they were preparing for bed that evening that the three boys had an opportunity to further discuss the afternoon's incident.

"Is your horse OK?" Terry asked, kicking off his shoes.

"Yes," Jim answered. "As long as he didn't get a big drink of water he—Oh, golly!"

"What's the matter?" the other two asked, aroused at the dismay in Jim's tone.

"I've lost my belt," Jim returned. "I had it on when I went to the corral, and I guess I must have dropped it there. I'll have to go back and find it."

"You've got to have it for inspection tomorrow," said Don. "Wait a shake, and I'll go back with you."

"No, you won't," vetoed Jim. "I can sneak out myself and make the trip in record time. No use in running the risk of having you reported with me. Douglas is patrolling post Number Five and I can slip through him."

"Yes, but the guard will have been changed by the time you get back," Terry reminded him. "Then what are you going to do?"

"I'll just have to take my chances and slip through while he is at the far end of the patrol," replied Jim, putting his shirt on again. "I should have seen to it that I didn't drop my belt, that's all. You fellows go to sleep, and I'll soon be back."

"OK," agreed Don. "Good luck, kid!"

"Thanks," murmured Jim, looking carefully from the flap of the tent. "See you later."

With that he was gone, slipping back of the tents and keeping well in the shadows. At the edge of the camp he waited until he saw Douglas standing with his back toward him. Then Jim slipped by him and plunged into the woods.

It didn't take him long to reach the spot where the horses were corralled and after a little hunting he found his belt. It had dropped close to the foot of a clump of bushes and was out of the direct rays of the moon. Buckling it around his waist Jim began his return journey to the camp.

But now, as he approached the place, he became very cautious. He must trust to luck to slip past the man at the post and it would be no easy task.

He decided that perhaps by flitting along past the animals he could more easily gain the corner of the nearest company street and by lying on his stomach in the shadow of a tent he could escape the eyes of the cadet until it was safe to move on. With this thought in mind Jim moved to the horses and then paused.

There was a tall white shape close to the animals, and they had sensed the presence of the thing. It looked to be a very tall man shrouded in white, and he was at the moment near the foremost horses. Forgetting his unusual position Jim rushed forward to see what was going on.

The shape before him heard his quick step, turned toward him, and then moved with an agility that astonished the cadet captain. Slapping the flanks of the horses right and left the man in white started them moving. Jim jumped forward.

"Hey, you!" he cried. "What are you doing to those horses?"

The figure in white took to the trees swiftly and Jim was unable to stop him. For the horses, frightened by something, perhaps the white shape itself, moved with increasing speed out of the corral. Before Jim could call to them it had developed into a wild stampede, and the horses were headed like a cyclone for the nearest tents.

# CHAPTER 6

## THE TROUBLE BUG BITES DEEP

After that, things happened rapidly. Just as the horses began their rapid flight the sentry on the post rushed up to Jim. As luck would have it, it was none other than Rowen.

Before he could say anything the stampeding horses hit the first tents. They had spread out fanwise on their wild run, and those on the wings were unable to push into the company streets. Blindly they crashed into the tents, taking two of them down in a flash and tipping a third over. The thunder of hoofs, the ripping of tent cords and the shouts of bewildered cadets buried under the entangling canvas turned the peaceful camp into a raging scene of chaos.

Cadets at the further end of the camp ran out, only to meet the galloping horses face to face. They were too bewildered to comprehend at once just what was going on, but they scurried back under cover. There was a vast uproar on all sides. A cloud of dust rose over the camp, partially obscuring the moon. To add to the confusion the sentries on other posts excitedly fired their guns.

Jim stood confused, wiping the dust from his eyes impatiently. Close beside him stood Rowen, coughing violently from the dust that the horses had raised. When he could speak he turned to Jim sternly.

"What are you doing here, Mercer?" he asked.

"I went back to the corral for my belt and then I saw a white shape near the horses," related Jim. "Just as I challenged him he slapped them on the flank, starting the stampede."

Rowen looked around the near-by woods. There was nothing to be seen. Deliberately he faced Jim.

"Absurd, Mercer," he declared, his intention plain.

"Do you mean you think I'm lying?" Jim demanded, his cheeks flushing.

"I don't have to mean anything. You tell me a story like that but I don't see the faintest evidence of it. What do you expect of me?"

"Look here, Rowen," said Jim. "How far away were you when these horses started?"

"A few yards. I was just patrolling this way when I heard them go," answered the sentry.

"Then you heard me say, 'What are you doing to those horses?' didn't you?"

"No, Mercer, I did not," returned Rowen, steadily.

"You did so!" retorted Jim, flatly.

"I heard nothing," repeated Rowen. "When I got here I found the horses in flight and I saw you standing back of them. Under the circumstances I must tell that to the proper officers and the colonel."

"Certainly you must. But I will also tell them about the white shape."

"I hope they will be a little more inclined to believe you than I am," sneered Rowen.

Jim took a step forward. "Rowen, if you intimate that I lie, I'll surely thrash you worse than I did this afternoon!"

"Mercer, in addition to reporting you for stampeding the horses, I shall also report you for threatening the sentry while he was performing his duty," followed up the vengeful cadet.

Hot words leaped to Jim's lips, but he stopped them. More words would lead to trouble, and he was sure that he had enough of that on his hands right now to last him for some time. Beside that, the camp was a bedlam and the horses were scattered all over the meadow below. Outwardly cool he faced the sentry.

"I am going to help round up the horses," he told Rowen. "I'll see you later."

With this Jim turned and ran across the camp, heading down the slope to the field below. The colonel was now on the job, with some realization of what had occurred. A detail of cadets was busy at the fallen tents, lifting the canvas and helping the stunned soldiers out into the open. One boy had had his shoulder sprained but that was all the physical damage there was. Most of the horses had halted on the plain below and were quietly cropping the grass.

All of the cavalrymen turned instinctively toward the horses and were now engaged in the difficult job of trying to secure them. The infantrymen and artillerymen stood around talking things over, understanding that there had been a stampede but not fully realizing why the horses had run away.

"Guess something just scared them and they bolted," Cadet Douglas said, speaking to a group.

"I'd like to know where Jim is?" said Terry.

"Too bad it had to happen while he was out of the camp," returned Don, in a low voice. "If the colonel ever learns that he was absent at the time he'll have a job explaining where he was. If he doesn't turn up and go hunting the horses he'll have to answer for that."

Drill Master Rhodes bore down on the assembled cadets. "A few fires to be lighted, please," he directed briskly. At this word the cadets scattered and fell to work gathering fuel for fires. A short time later a half-dozen fires lighted up the sky and threw the camp into bright relief.

"There's Jim!" cried Don, pulling at Terry's sleeve. "He has been right on the job."

Jim was riding Squall bareback and driving other horses before him. Lieutenant Thompson brought in others, and the main band of the animals had been captured. But there were now at least five horses that had run far off and some of the cadets saddled and went after them.

This time they found real work cut out for them. The horses that had run the farthest away were the unruly ones. They objected strongly to being captured and led the cadets a merry chase. After an hour of hard work all but one horse had been captured.

"Mr. Mercer," called the colonel. "Take Mr. Thompson and get that one stray horse."

Jim and Thompson mounted and dashed across the field toward Twinkletoes, the stubborn cavalry horse. The animal, a beautiful chestnut stallion, tossed his head disdainfully and trotted off in a sweeping circle, seeming to enjoy the chase keenly. He was moving away from the camp and Jim saw that unless he could get on the far side of the horse he would lose him. Accordingly, he abandoned the direct chase, heading Squall out across the moonlit field until he had passed the cavorting horse. Then Jim swung sharply in toward the camp, the animal now in front of him. Thompson stopped and allowed Twinkletoes to retreat past him, and then the two cavalry officers began a chase that entertained and delighted the camp.

Twinkletoes tried in vain to dodge out of the circle which the two young soldiers had drawn around him, and it took all of their skill to keep him from attaining his objective. Twinkletoes raced and plunged, first toward one side and then toward the other, making short, mad little dashes, but as fast as he dashed the officers dashed after him. In this fashion, working ever in toward the slope, the two cadets drove the frisky animal in far enough to make escape possible only by dashing up the hill. This Twinkletoes refused to do, and Jim, staking all on a last desperate drive, forced Squall up beside the fugitive horse and secured him. As he led him into camp a cheer went up.

"Very good work, men," nodded the colonel.

The horses were now all in and the work of securing them firmly went on. No recall was sounded and the cadets wandered aimlessly around the camp. When Jim and the other cavalrymen returned to the central fire they found the colonel standing there, surrounded by the instructors and most of the cadets. Jim was walking toward the colonel to make his report when Rowen stepped from the group, triumph written on his face.

"Mr. Mercer!" he called, loudly. All of the assembled soldiers, including the colonel, turned to look at him.

"What is it, Mr. Rowen?" Jim asked, quietly.

"You will kindly consider yourself under arrest for starting the stampede!" said Rowen, still in the loud voice.

His words produced a decided sensation. The colonel looked particularly astonished. Terry groaned and nudged Don.

"What do you know about that! Jim started the stampede!"

"Mr. Mercer, did you start the stampede?" the colonel asked.

"No, sir," replied Jim, promptly.

The colonel turned to Rowen. "What is your exact charge against Captain Mercer, Mr. Rowen?" he asked.

"I charge Captain Mercer with being absent from camp without official leave, of stampeding the horses, and of threatening a sentry in the performance of his duty!" cried Rowen.

"Those are very serious charges, Captain Mercer," the colonel told Jim. "What have you to say to them?"

"I admit being out of camp without leave, but refuse to acknowledge stampeding the horses or having been in any way responsible for their breaking loose. I did threaten to thrash

Mr. Rowen because he insisted that I was deliberately lying when I informed him that a figure clothed entirely in white slapped the horses and started them on their stampede," reported Jim. There was a stir of eager interest from the cadets.

"A figure in white?" said the colonel, sharply. "What was that, Captain Mercer?"

"I do not know, sir," replied Jim. "I challenged him sharply and at the sound of my voice he slapped the horses on the flanks, starting them on their break."

"Captain Mercer says he called out to the figure in white/" said the colonel, turning to Rowen. "Did you hear him call, Mr. Rowen?"

"I did not, sir," answered the sentry. "Colonel Morrell, Captain Mercer did not call out!"

"Limit your statement to the fact that you did not hear him, Mr. Rowen," advised the colonel. Rowen flushed and trembled with rage.

"And you really saw a white shape at the horses, Captain Mercer? This talk of ghosts has not influenced you any, has it?"

"Not a bit, sir," affirmed Jim, gravely. "I distinctly heard the sharp sounds of his slaps and as I started for him he glided into the woods close at hand."

"Did you see anything, Mr. Rowen?" the colonel asked.

"The only thing I saw was Mr. Mercer standing there, watching the horses tear across the camp, sir," answered Rowen.

The colonel thought for a moment. "Very well, men," he returned. "I will consider the case carefully. Captain Mercer, you will consider yourself at least temporarily under arrest, on the two charges preferred by Mr. Rowen, namely, for being absent without official leave and for threatening the sentry, although I realize that you threatened Mr. Rowen not for ordering your arrest, but for doubting your word. All these things don't go well with an officer's commission, Captain Mercer, and I shall be compelled to look into the entire affair."

"Very good, sir," responded Jim, saluting.

The cadets were sent back to their cots and soon quiet settled over the entire camp. In their tent Jim, Terry and Don discussed the situation.

"Just your luck to run right into Rowen," commented Terry. "I'd like to bet my last nickel that he heard you call out, too."

"I think that he did, but we can't prove it," sighed Jim. "Well, I'm not going to worry about it—"

"You won't need to," reassured Don. "The colonel will see to it that you have the proper justice. Your word is as good as Rowen's and he will find out the truth some way."

# CHAPTER 7

## THE OLD MAN OF THE RIDGE

Jim's punishment did not last long. A circumstance came up that made the colonel suspend judgment for some time.

One morning, soon after the incidents related, a man in a battered old car drove up to the camp. He was a minister who preached in a regular circuit of county churches and he was known to the colonel. The headmaster received him with great pleasure and the two men talked of many things as they sat in the colonel's tent.

"By the way," said the Reverend Mr. Powers, after a time. "Did someone go past your camp very hurriedly a few nights ago?"

The colonel showed signs of unusual interest. "Why, yes, a few nights ago a wagon with two men in it tore right through the camp," he said. "We couldn't stop it."

"There was a man and a boy in it," corrected the pastor. "Well, then you don't know what sent them flying past you like that?"

"No," confessed the colonel. "If you had seen the way they flew by, you wouldn't wonder that I didn't learn anything about them. But tell me what you know."

"First, I would like to ask you a question. Have you heard anything about a ghost of the Ridge, since you have been here?"

The colonel snorted. "I haven't heard much about anything else," he retorted.

"The ghost scared these two off. The father is a farmer who came down here from Pennsylvania. As it turns out, he is very superstitious, and the very first night on his own farm, while driving into the yard with his only son, he saw the white shape skulking along near his barn. He was just about crazed with fear and fled to the valley, passing your camp as he did."

"Of course this ghost is simply some would-be humorous person who is having some fun," was the colonel's opinion. But Mr. Powers had another opinion.

"I doubt that very much, Morrell. The thing has been going on for years and some very good citizens have given up their homes just on account of it. The joke would have worn out years ago. No, I'm inclined to think that there is something deeper in it than mere fun."

"Some determined effort should be made to drive the ghost from the Ridge," grumbled the headmaster.

"Who is to start it?" shrugged the parson. "No one seems to want to and the sheriff of the county simply laughs at the whole business."

As a result of this talk the colonel called Rowen and Jim into his tent after drill that very afternoon. They faced him expectantly.

"Gentlemen," said the colonel. Then he paused, and a frown swept over his face. "I call you gentlemen, and will continue to do so until one of you is proved guilty of deliberate lying. Your conflicting stories show that one of your statements, coming from one or the other of you, is a deliberate falsehood. But to get back to the business in hand: I have just heard some more tales concerning this ghost of the Ridge, and in view of it I have decided to drop the suspension against Captain Mercer. The word of one of you is as good to me as the word of the other, and until I prove that one of you is trying to conceal anything I must consider the case dismissed until further notice. Mr. Rowen, you say you did not hear Mr. Mercer call out nor did you see the white shape. But on the other hand, Captain Mercer did tell you immediately that he had seen a white shape, and that the ghost—or whatever it was—had started the stampede. Inasmuch as you did not see Captain Mercer start the stampede, and you doubted his word, I shall be able to hold him only on the count of being absent without official leave. For that Captain Mercer will receive demerits. It that all clear, and satisfactory?"

"Very much so, to me, sir," approved Jim. Rowen muttered.

"What was that, Mr. Rowen?" the colonel asked, sharply.

Rowen lost his temper in his sudden fright. "I simply said that of course a Mercer would get the breaks, sir!" he sneered. Then, realizing the slip he had made, his face turned white.

"So!" murmured the colonel. His eyes flashed but his voice was calm. "I asked you if my decision was satisfactory, Mr. Rowen."

"Yes, sir," murmured the disappointed cadet.

"Very well. You are both dismissed," nodded the colonel. Left alone, his brain worked busily. He saw a good many things in a clear light now.

"Petty jealousy, and he is trying to revenge him self on Mercer," thought the little colonel. "I guess I can pretty well tell which one of those young men is lying!"

On the following morning, when the Orders of the Day were read, Jim and his friends were delighted to hear in the crisp voice of the battalion orderly that the charges brought against Captain Mercer by Sentry Rowen were to be temporarily dismissed, with the exception of the charge of leaving camp unofficially, for which Captain Mercer was to receive twenty-five demerits.

A hundred demerits were sufficient to send a man home from the encampment and two hundred at school would dismiss any cadet permanently.

That afternoon there was a partial holiday and the cadets set out to enjoy themselves. It was a mild and warm afternoon, with a fleecy sky overhead, through which the sun peeped at intervals. Don and Jim sat in the tent, trying to decide just what to do.

"What do you say to a hike over the Ridge, a sort of exploring trip?" was Don's suggestion.

"Sounds good," approved Jim. "Who can we get to go along with us?"

"We'll scout around and find out," announced Don, getting up from his cot.

After looking up their most intimate friends they found that only Terry and Raoul Vench cared to go tramping.

"We'll be glad to go along," yawned the redhead. He and Raoul had been idly watching the swimmers when Jim and Don found them. "I'm weary of doing nothing!"

"Too lazy to do anything but watch the other fellows swim around and enjoy themselves, is that it?" asked Jim.

"Yes, but you see, I enjoy it that way," returned Terry, seriously. "I have a vivid imagination and in time, by concentrating on the swimmers, I too feel the cool of the water and the exhilaration of the exercise. Just requires a little imaginative concentration, Jimmie my friend."

"You're a wonderful fellow," glowed Jim. "Just you imagine me a couple of ice-cream sodas, will you?"

"Pay me first!" said Terry with a grin. "Money back if I fail to come across."

The four cadets set out at a brisk pace up the slope of the Ridge. It was heavily wooded and every now and then they came across a clearing in which a farmhouse could be seen. They were not long in reaching the very top of the series of hills called Rustling Ridge and they paused to look down into the opposite valley from the one above which their camp was pitched.

"Nice picture," observed Terry. "Why do they call this place Rustling Ridge?"

"In the fall, when the wind blows hard, the leaves rustle, and from that fact comes the name," Don volunteered.

"How'd you learn that?" Vench wanted to know.

"I asked a farm boy who was watching us play baseball the other day," replied the infantry lieutenant.

"Look at that old house up there," called out Jim, pointing to a huge square structure that showed a battered roof with leaning chimneys over the tops of the trees. "Looks like a fitting habitation for the ghost of this place."

"Just about," agreed Vench. "But that little cabin down below looks better to me, because I bet we can get a good drink at the place. Let's go down."

The others agreed and they tramped down the side of the slope toward a plain little cabin, constructed of unpainted boards, with a roofed front porch on it. At some distance below them they could see the largest town in the county.

"What town is that?" asked Jim.

"I think that must be Rideway," replied Don.

Reaching the cabin they rounded the corner, to halt suddenly as they saw a figure there. It was a little old man in a wheelchair, a man with sparse gray hair, sallow cheeks, and a few good teeth remaining. His eyes were keen and penetrating and he was puffing in evident enjoyment on a huge pipe.

He greeted them readily enough. "Hi, there, boys, step right up," he shrilled, in a rasping voice. "Soldiers, eh? You look pretty young. Where you stationed?"

"We aren't soldiers of the United States Army," Don told him. "We are cadets from Woodcrest Military Institute, and we're camping over on the other side of the Ridge. We were passing by and thought we'd drop in for a drink of water."

"Thought you were too young-looking for regular soldiers," nodded the old man, taking in every detail of their uniforms. "Want a drink of good water, eh?"

"Yes," Don replied. "But we wouldn't want to trouble you any."

"Oh, hush up!" was the good-natured reply. "I know that you're thinking I'm out of commission and I can't help you. Just sit down on the porch here and see how old Peter Vancouver does it." With that the old man gave the right wheel of his chair a whirl and to the astonishment of the boys shot himself around in a half circle and in through the open door. From there they saw him roll across the room and vanish through the door of another room.

"My gosh!" breathed Terry. "Can't he work that buggy of his!"

"Probably years of practice has made him proficient," said Don, softly.

With the same bewildering speed and dexterity the man returned in his chair, holding a pitcher and a tin cup in his hand. Even while in motion he poured the water out.

He seemed to enjoy watching the boys drink deeply, and when they had finished he wheeled back to the kitchen and returned at lightning speed. Noting the interested looks of the boys he chuckled.

"Guess the old man knows how to walk well's if he had feet, eh?"

"You walk better than a whole lot of people who have feet," gravely affirmed Vench.

"If you was spending your life in one of these all-fired things you'd know how to ride one, too," he told them. "Don't you fellows go. I don't see a heap of folks and I like to chin once in a while."

"We'll be glad to stay and talk with you, Mr. Vancouver." Jim smiled, leaning back against a post. "We are just out exploring and we'd just as soon sit here and talk as wander around."

"Glad to hear you say it," said the old man.

"Let's hear something about that there camp of yours."

The boys told him several things about the camp, all of which seemed to interest him deeply. In the course of the talk the incident of the ghost and the stampede was mentioned. The old man bent eagerly forward.

"Did you get a visit from the ghost?" he cried.

"Yes, he stampeded our horses," Jim told him. "What do you know about him, Mr. Vancouver?"

The man chuckled. "All a poor old invalid would know about such like he hears," the man replied. "I ain't never seen the thing, but I heard plenty. Raises old Ned in the hills here, and has been at it for years."

"If we get a chance we are going to nail him good," Don promised.

"Good idea," Mr. Vancouver approved. "Blasted business has been driving people off the Ridge for years. Wouldn't be surprised if the fellow drove you cadets home."

"Drive us out of camp!" cried Vench, stirring.

"He might!" the old man said.

"He'll have to go some to do that," snorted Terry. "He'll be lucky if we don't steal his best nightgown right off him!"

"Getting late, fellows," warned Don. "We had better be getting back. Thanks a lot for your good drink of water, Mr. Vancouver, and we've enjoyed being with you."

"Enjoyed being able to talk to you boys," he returned heartily. "Come up again some time."

"We'll be glad to," promised the boys, as they started off. Mr. Vancouver called a final word after them.

"You had better keep your eyes open for that cussed ghost! No tellin' when he'll pop up and scare the life out of you!"

The cadets laughed good-naturedly and walked at a rapid pace up the side of the Ridge. The sun was going down in the west and they would have to keep up a good stride in order to arrive in time for supper.

"Interesting old fellow, that Vancouver," Jim observed.

"He surely is," Vench agreed. "We'll have to chat with him some other time."

"Too bad he can't move around—that is, walk around," Don said. "As a matter of fact, he does move around mighty fast, but I mean it is a shame he can't go walking around, same as you and me."

"Like everybody else around here, he believes that dog-gone ghost is the last word in efficiency," growled Terry. "I guess the real trouble is that nobody dares to put on a real hunt for the ghost. Fellows, we'll have to make it our business to run down that ghost!"

"If it pops up again soon, we will," Don promised.

# CHAPTER 8

## MOVING FLAME

For a week or more there were no unusual events. Camping life went on calmly, the drill and fun occupying the days in regular succession. By this time all of the boys were enjoying themselves to the utmost. Muscles were limber and strong, bodies straight and vigorous, and the appetites outrageous.

"We certainly are keeping the cooks hustling," Terry chuckled one day in the mess tent. "I'm going for another helping of beans."

But when the genial redhead went to the kitchen tent he was firmly but politely refused. "Nothing doing, Mr. Mackson," said the mess sergeant, firmly. "You've already had three plates full and that is the allotment."

"No more beans for a starving man?" Terry inquired, in dismay.

"No more for you anyway. I don't know why you should be starving, I'm sure."

"All right," returned the red-headed one, calmly. "My mother will get even with you!"

"What do you mean, your mother will?" cried the cook, staring.

"When my body is shipped home, and she learns that her darling boy starved to death in the camp, she will spend the rest of her life calling down vengeance upon the head of the hard-headed and hard-hearted cook that turned him away with tears in his eyes!" was the answer. The mess tent shook with the laugh that went up. But the cook was prepared to answer him back.

"You're right about the cook turning him away with tears in his eyes," the cook said. "It brings tears to my eyes to see the hole in the bean pile when you get eating!"

Terry retired thoughtfully, paying no heed to the mocking gibes which greeted him on all sides. After a moment he looked at Vench, who was eating across the table from him. Vench had just pushed his plate to one side.

"How many plates of beans did you have, Raoul?" Terry whispered.

"Two was enough for me," returned the little one.

"My son, heaven's blessings upon you! Just take my plate and hit the trail for the cook!"

Mr. Vench took Terry's plate and gravely approached the cook. But as soon as that worthy saw the particular dent in the tin plate he shook his head wisely.

"Nothing doing, Mr. Vench," he said. "That is Mackson's plate. You don't work that game here!"

"Thank you, sir!" Vench murmured, while the cadets enjoyed the failure of the move to the utmost. With that Vench turned away. But at that moment the cook was called to the far end of the mess tent. With swiftness that was commendable Vench reached over the stove and heaped the plate. Then he sped back to the delighted Terry.

"Ram that in your musket and keep still!" he said, as he took his place.

Terry needed no second invitation. He dug into the pile of beans with alacrity. And in a moment the sharp voice of the cook reached him.

"Mr. Mackson, where did you get those beans?"

Terry looked blank. "I am not at all sure, sir," he answered, politely. "I had just turned my back, and when I looked around there they were, right under my nose!"

"Did you come and take them while I was not looking?" cried the cook.

"Haven't been out of my seat since you broke my heart with your refusal," was the answer. "And you didn't give any to Mr. Vench, so it is up to you to figure out how I got the beans!"

"Bring them here, Mr. Mackson!" said the mess sergeant.

Terry shoveled the last forkful into his mouth. "Beg pardon?" he asked blandly.

"I'll put you on report!" growled the sergeant.

"My dear fellow, you can't," smiled Terry. "I didn't take them myself and so you have no charge to prefer. And if you did I'd pound all the beans out of you once I got you away from the mess tent!"

"That amounts to threatening an officer while on duty, Mr. Mackson!" charged the sergeant.

"That's not a threat, that's a promise," grinned the redhead. The sergeant muttered savagely but subsided.

"Much obliged," Terry whispered to Vench. "Some day I'll help you out."

"But not in the matter of beans," smiled Vench. "They just don't happen to be my weakness!"

One of the steady visitors to the camp was the little Carson boy. He was the son of the farmer from whom the camp supplies were purchased, and the cadets had taken a great liking to him. He was a friendly, likable boy and obviously deeply interested in the activities of the young soldiers. He watched all of their maneuvers with fascinated interest and the cadets welcomed him in their tents.

"That youngster has the makings of a good cadet in him," Don said. "Too bad he isn't one of us. How would you like to be a cadet, Jimmie?"

The boy flushed with pleasure and looked around the tent. "I'd like it more than anything else in the world," he told them. "I'll tell you a secret. Want to hear it?"

"Well, if it isn't too deep for us, we would," Jim assured him.

"I'm saving my money to go to Woodcrest," the little fellow confided. "Guess how much I have saved already?"

"I can't imagine, but I hope it is a lot," replied Don.

"It is!" was the eager retort. "I have a dollar and fifty-seven cents toward it!"

"That's great!" said Terry promptly. "You'll need a little more than that, but it is a good beginning, anyway. Just you keep on going."

"I'll surely be glad when I get a uniform like you have," the boy went on, wistfully. "I think they're swell."

There were other boys who drifted to the camp but they did not attract the attention of the cadets as much as the Carson boy did. They came to look around and fool a bit and in time most of them were chased away. But Jimmie Carson was never in the way and so he was allowed to come often to camp.

One afternoon a group of cadets went for another hike over the Ridge and on the way back they passed the Carson farm. Jimmie called to them to come in and they did so. To their delight Mrs. Carson, a plain, kindly woman of middle age, insisted that they try a huge apple pie that she had made.

"Don't give any to Terry, Mrs. Carson," begged Jim, as they sat on the back porch. Don, Jim, Terry, Douglas and Vench were there at the time.

"Why is that? Doesn't he feel well?" the farmer's wife inquired, anxiously.

"He has had stomach trouble for a long time," returned Jim, gravely. "The doctor said that of all things in the world, he mustn't eat apple pie!"

"I'll tell you what it is, Mrs. Carson," spoke up the persecuted one, before anything else could be said. "I have a falling stomach and I can't seem to locate the bottom at any time. But I'm sure that if I can only have a slice of that apple pie, I'll surely plug up the floor of my stomach and have no more trouble!"

"Of all the left-handed compliments in the world!" gasped Douglas. "He must think your pie is some kind of cement with which to secure his stomach. Tell a lady that her pie will plug him up!"

Mrs. Carson laughed heartily. "I guess there is nothing the matter with any of you boys," she said. "Try my pie and see if it is like cement!"

"I could die of embarrassment!" murmured Terry, as he bit into his piece of pie. "But this pie will surely revive me."

The farmer himself came up and talked to the boys for a time. The unexpected arrival of the soldiers on the Ridge and the subsequent contract to supply them with fresh food had done wonders for the poor farmer and his family. A good many dollars were coming his way from the camp down the slope.

"Here is the baby of the family," smiled Mrs. Carson, appearing a little later with a pretty little girl of six. The cadets promptly forgot all else in their efforts to amuse and entertain Dorothy Carson. It was late before they headed back to camp, after thanking the farmer's wife for the good time they had had.

"I've had pie before," murmured Terry. "But never such pie as that!"

"Is that so?" asked Jim. "Well, it is a cinch that Don and I can't believe anything you say hereafter!"

"Why not?"

"Because one time at our house you said the same thing about my mother's pie," said Jim.

"But don't forget, this pie helped his stomach!" said Vench, slyly. "Probably your mother's pie didn't plug up the bottom of his stomach!"

"If I ever speak again, it will be to myself, and in a dark room," sighed Terry.

They had not been back in the tent long before the Officer of the Guard appeared at the tent with a list in his hand. "Lieutenant Mercer, you will report for guard duty at Post Number Three at twelve o'clock," he informed Don.

"Very good, sir," Don saluted.

At midnight Lieutenant Don reported to the sentry at the far end of the camp, at a point near the farm belonging to the Hyde family. After an exchange of instructions he took the post, waiting for the call. It came soon after.

"Sentry, Post Two," someone said near to him. Don faced toward the sentry who was next to him. "Sentry, Post Three," he called. Number Four passed the report call on until eight sentries had reported. Then they began their pacing up and down on their patrols.

Don's stretch was a long one, extending from the edge of the camp at the company street to a point back of the horse corral. At no time did he meet the sentry who patrolled Post Four. Just at the time Don reached the place where Post Four joined his post the other sentry was at the far end of his stretch, and when Don had returned to the company street Number Four was at the beginning of his post patrol. In this way there was no likelihood of sentries stopping to chat and no huge gaps left in the line of patrol duty.

The moon was a mere slice but the stars were bright pinheads in the sky. The air was warm and heavy with the smell of the woods. Don enjoyed his patrol thoroughly. At twelve-thirty he looked up the Ridge casually. Toward the top he saw a tiny jet of flame, right above the Hyde place.

"Looks like somebody striking a match," he reflected, pacing slowly.

Then he stopped quickly. The jet of flame sprang up rapidly. Something was burning, flaring up into a huge ball of roaring fire. And as Don looked, completely at a loss, this mass of flame moved with ever increasing speed down the hill toward the Hyde house!

# CHAPTER 9

## SHARP WORK AS FIRE FIGHTERS

Don stood spellbound while the huge ball of fire rolled down on the Hyde place. There was a crash that he could hear plainly even at his distance and the burning ball hit the barn. In a twinkling of an eye the wooden structure caught fire.

Then Don came to life. Raising his rifle he fired three swift shots, waking the camp instantly.

The Officer of the Guard rushed up to him. "What is the trouble, Lieutenant?" the cadet panted. But a red glow in the sky told him the story at once.

"Report a large fire at that farmhouse," said Don. The Officer of the Guard dug for the colonel.

By this time the cadet camp was well lighted by the glare from Hyde's barn. The colonel saw that hard work was needed and he directed the bugler to sound assembly. This was done, and the half-dressed cadets fell in formation.

"Secure all pails and double-quick it to the farmhouse!" was the order. The colonel knew that in this rural area there was no organized fire department and whatever attempts were made to extinguish a fire always came from helpful neighbors. Instantly, the ranks broke and the commissary department was fairly turned upside down as the soldiers rummaged for pails. When these had been secured they raced down the company street and took the road to Hyde's house.

Fortunately for them—and for the Hydes—the distance was short. When the first cadets arrived in the front yard the barn was a roaring furnace. Hyde and his two sons were running around the yard in an aimless fashion and as Jim and Terry arrived the three of them dashed into the blazing barn. A moment later they came out, each of them hanging onto squealing, thrashing horses.

"The horses!" cried Jim, and at the word the cavalrymen and the artillerymen formed a body around him. In a mass they rushed the door of the barn. Fighting their way inside past the Hydes, who were coming out, the cadets paused to look about the stable, gasping as the heavy smoke crowded down their lungs.

The inside of the barn was curiously lighted. A pall of heavy smoke hung in the structure, and through this curtain the dull red flames shone and licked. Snapping and crackling sounds reached their ears as the wood burned, and a terrible shrieking, from the terrified horses, went right through them. Blind with fear the animals kicked and screamed.

No word was spoken as the cadets made a rush for the nearest horses. Jim had not put on a shirt, but some of the others had and these they now whipped off, throwing them over the heads of the rearing animals. Jim scooped a blanket up from the rack as he passed and made a cast for the head of a big dray horse in a stall.

But now his troubles began. The horse, wild with fright, avoided the blanket. It kicked at Jim and even snapped, tearing frantically on its halter. The heat was cracking Jim's skin, the smoke choked him, and the crazy horse made his head ache trying to follow his rapid movements. Worse than that, the halter was tied in a ring on the wall, and the cavalryman was unable to pull it loose. As he was ready to sob with anger his fingers closed over the catch and with a jerk that tore his skin he loosed the rearing horse. Like a flash the animal backed from its stall and tried to find the door.

Now Jim succeeded in getting the blanket over his head and he felt his way to the door. The first breath of fresh air that he got went through him like the stab of a sword. Stumbling at every step he led the trembling horse to a tree far away from the barn and tied him securely. The smell of burning hair jabbed his nose and he knew that the animal had been burned in more than one place.

"I've got to go back," he gasped, gulping the air in huge draughts. "But I can't, I just can't!"

But he started back, his feet like lead and his head ready to burst. Before he reached the door of the barn, however, a blackened figure with red hair stopped him.

"They're all out," Terry shouted. "And I'm all in!"

Together they sank down on the rude back steps of the farmhouse, entirely played out. While they sat there the bucket brigade was in full swing.

Those cadets who had been fortunate enough to secure buckets had jumped into action without wasting a moment's time. The vanguard found the well and began to pump vigorously. As soon as the first pail was filled it was passed from hand to hand and the last cadet, running as close to the fire as the heat would allow him to, tossed it on the blaze. By the time he had finished a second cadet had run forward with another pail full. A second contingent of cadets, impatient at waiting around the well, found a small creek back of the barn and the buckets were dipped in here. Two steady streams were now being played in splashes on the blaze.

There was no hope of saving the barn but the work went grimly forward. A mountain of sparks was ascending, threatening the house and the smaller structures near by, to say nothing of the fields and woods. It required a special corps to put out scores of small fires that jumped up in the fields and on the other buildings. But in time the splashing buckets of water kept the sparks down and although the barn burned to the ground the house and smaller buildings were saved.

It seemed to the cadets that they had been working for hours on their task. Numerous neighbors had run over from near-by farms, armed with buckets and blankets, and their assistance was a welcome help. A wheezing old hand-pump on a flat truck was finally run into the yard and the water from the creek was thrown in a more or less uncertain stream on the smoldering embers of the ruins, but had the Hydes been compelled to wait for it and for the neighbors they would have been burned out of the house and home. Clouds of hissing steam rose from the blackened wood as the water was pumped and thrown on it.

Jim and Terry had braced up sufficiently to join the bucket brigade and they passed the pails with the others. Some of the cadets had stormed in the back door of Hyde's house and had located a few pails and pans. As for the father and his two sons they had not been of much use after the horses had been taken. Utterly bewildered by the swift events they had run from place to place, too shaken to do anything practical.

"Were all of the animals taken out?" the colonel asked the farmer. He nodded dully.

"Wasn't nothing but horses in that barn," he returned. "The chickens is in the run there."

The unfortunate chickens were scorched by the heat which had been so near to them but all of them were alive. They had run around the long inclosure squawking and screeching but the damage had not touched them. Some pigs near by were safe enough, and the only thing which had suffered was the barn itself and the horses, most of whom were burned in patches. Jim, who had recovered from his experience, dispatched a man to the camp to bring soothing salve for the animals' burns. This was done and under Jim and Thompson's watchful eyes the scorches were tenderly glossed over to heal.

A large group had gathered around the farmer and his sons and the cadets. One of the neighbors asked how the fire had started. Hyde shrugged his shoulders.

"I dunno," he said. "All of a sudden I waked up to see the fire and we run out in a jiffy. I didn't see how it got afire."

The colonel turned to Don, who was close by. "How did you happen to see this fire, Lieutenant Mercer?" he asked.

Don narrated the story of the moving flame. The neighbors shot inquiring looks at the Hydes. A dozen tongues formed the word "Maul."

"Maul is dead," said one of the sons. "How could he do it?"

"Don't forget the ghost of the Ridge," said a man, seriously. "That's Maul's ghost."

The oldest son had been prowling about the ruins and now set up a cry. "Look-a-here, Pop," he called. There was an instant rush to the rear of the barn.

In the dim light of a few lanterns they made out the charred outline of wheels and under a smoking board some wisps of straw. A murmur of comprehension went up.

"Loaded a wagon of hay and lighted her up," shouted a farmer. "Then they rolled it down the hill at the barn."

There was no doubt that such had been the case. And no one seemed to ask why, a fact that puzzled the colonel and the boys.

"Why should anyone do a thing like that? And who is this Maul?" the colonel asked.

None of the Hydes replied but a neighbor was willing to talk. "A few years back there was a hill feud between the Hydes and the Mauls," he said. "One or the other of them was trying to drive the other family out. But all of the Mauls disappeared or died several years ago. This here ghost must be one of the Mauls!"

"Evidently a very real Maul, if he can load a wagon with hay and roll it down the hill," replied the colonel dryly. "Captain Jordan!"

"Sir?" the senior captain replied.

"Take a detail of men and search the hill. If you find anyone that looks suspicious bring him here to me."

"Very well, sir," replied Jordan, and picked a detail of five men. They departed up the slope at once.

"You won't find any ghost hanging around now," grinned a toothless old man.

The colonel paid no attention to the old man and they hung around for an hour longer. It was now three o'clock, but no one thought of quitting the scene. From snatches of conversation the cadets learned more about the bitter feud that had existed for generations between the Hydes and the Mauls. The last Maul had been drowned in a near-by river.

"At least he was swept down the river in a flood," a neighbor said. "Nobody ever saw him since."

"Well, these foolish feuds ought to stop," growled the colonel. "A lot of innocent people suffer because of them."

"We'll attend to our own affairs," the father said, sullenly. "We don't need any interfering."

"If it hadn't been for our interfering tonight you would have been without a dozen horses and your house, my friend," returned the colonel, calmly. The Hydes muttered to themselves.

Jordan and the detail returned soon afterward to report that there was no sign of anyone on the hill. "But we found the tracks and a lot of hay up on top of the hill."

There was now nothing to keep them there any longer and they went back to camp, tired but satisfied. There was no word of thanks from the farmer or his sons.

"Nice, grateful bunch," grumbled Don, inspecting sore hands and a red burn on his arm.

Jim ached all over but he managed to grin. "Sure, but we should worry. We got the horses out, and that is what counted."

# CHAPTER 10

## EMERGENCY SERVICE

THE drill was going on merrily. It was four days after the fire at the Hyde place and the cadets had recovered from the effects of their strenuous experience. On the day following the fire the colonel had ordered the suspension of the daily routine and a number of burns had been treated. Weary muscles and sore lungs had been rested to good advantage and now the swing of things was once more in evidence.

All of the units were having infantry drill. Even the cavalry and infantry divisions were compelled to drill with rifles every so often, and today, under Major Rhodes, a graduate of the school and one of the regular staff, they were hard at it. The sun beat down upon them from a clear sky but by this time the cadets were well used to it. The hottest days failed to shake them in their tasks.

Suddenly the colonel appeared and called the major. There was a hurried conference and then the major went back to his position. Crisply he called: "Battalion, attention! Count off in fours!"

The count ran along the line. At a further word the guns were dropped to rest and the cadets faced the colonel. He spoke to them in a ringing voice.

"Gentlemen of the Corps, we are faced with another call to duty. A good many serious things have happened while we have been here on the Ridge, but this is the most serious of them all. The little daughter of the farmer who supplies us with food has been lost or kidnapped!"

The closely packed ranks stirred. The colonel went on: "A number of organized groups are at present looking for this child all over the Ridge. We have not been asked to help, but of course it is our duty and we will form searching parties at once. There will be no more official duties until the child has been found or until some definite word has been received as to her whereabouts. I trust you will dutifully prosecute the search until every inch of the Ridge and the surrounding country has been scoured."

The colonel saluted the major and turned away. There was a total silence in the corps but eyes flashed with excitement.

"Companies dismissed," ordered Major Rhodes. The cadets broke ranks and stacked arms. From then on things moved fast. In groups the young soldiers formed for the search. It was decided that they would remain away from camp for the night if necessary, and knapsacks were hastily packed. While Don, Jim and Terry were preparing, Vench and Douglas hurried to their tent.

"Suppose we five form a bunch of our own," Douglas suggested.

"Sure," responded Don. "I think our best move would be to go to the Carson house and find out where the little girl was last seen. Then we can map out our campaign from that point."

This was agreed to and the cadets hurried off down the road. It was just noontime and they wanted to get in every bit of work they could while the daylight remained.

"That was the cute little girl we were playing with the day we had the pie," observed Vench, as they hurried along. "I certainly hope nothing has happened to her."

"I hope not," agreed Don. "It's possible that she just wandered off somewhere. Wonder who told the colonel about it?"

"Little Jimmie Carson," said Jim promptly. "I saw him come into camp just as we were leaving for drill."

It did not take them long to reach the Carson house, which they found to be thronged with visitors. Men from the neighboring houses had come to do their bit by searching and the strong Ridge women had come to console the heartbroken mother. Mrs. Carson was delighted to see the boys.

"Oh, you have come to help look for Dorothy?" she cried, seizing Don's hands.

"Our colonel has ordered the whole cadet corps to keep searching until we find the little one," Don smiled. "We have divided up in bands to scour the country."

"How very kind of your colonel—and of you!" cried the frightened woman. "With so many looking for the child I don't see why she shouldn't be found."

"Unless she's past finding!" said an old lady with a sad air and mournful eyes.

"She isn't past finding," snapped Jim, impatiently. "I haven't any doubt that we'll locate her. Now, Mrs. Carson, where was she last seen?"

"She went out last night about nine o'clock to bring in a rag doll that she had left out under the grape arbor," replied the farmer's wife. "I held the door open for her, so that she would surely find her way in, but she didn't, poor little soul. Oh, I'm so sorry that I ever let her go out. We searched the yard immediately, but we couldn't find a trace of her, and she didn't answer our calls."

"Thank you," said Don gently. "Then she disappeared from her own back yard?"

"Yes," nodded Mrs. Carson, wiping her eyes.

At that moment the county sheriff, a tall and disagreeable-looking man named Blount, swaggered into the room. It was evident that he regarded himself as the most important person there and as his eyes fell on the cadets his brow darkened.

"Humph!" he grunted. "So those soldier kids are looking too, eh? Well, they won't find anything."

Terry looked at the sheriff's shoes, and then allowed his eyes to travel slowly up the entire length of his body until he had seen all of him. The sheriff reddened and then blustered.

"Well, what's the matter with you?" he cried.

"Nothing," returned Terry, mildly. "I've never really seen an important man before and I wanted to get a good look now that I am close to one!"

"Say, I'll run you kids—" began the angry sheriff, as a slight snicker went up. But Don cut him short.

"Come on, you fellows," he called. "We have work to do. No use standing around wasting breath on useless subjects."

"Nice kindly old soul, that sheriff," growled Vench, when the cadets were again outside.

"He isn't worth thinking about," said Don. "Now, boys, let's get on the job."

Their first job was to look under the grape arbor, but scores of feet had churned up the ground so that nothing could be learned from it. They left the yard and struck off into the woods.

"Too bad we couldn't find a clue under the arbor," grumbled Terry.

"I doubt if there were any clues," advanced Jim. "Some of the men would have seen them in the first place. After all, we aren't detectives, and our job is to beat up the Ridge much in the manner of going over it with a fine-tooth comb."

"That is true," nodded Vench. "Suppose we don't run across her tonight? Are you going back to camp?"

"No," decided Don. "We'd only lose time. We'll stay here and get a fresh start early in the morning. The colonel wants us to stay right on the job until some trace of her is found."

"How are we to know if she is found?" Douglas asked.

"A cannon will be fired three times," replied Terry. "That's the signal for recall."

Throughout the entire afternoon and early evening the cadets tramped over the Ridge, going to parts of the rolling hills that they had never seen before. There was no sign of the little one, although they kept their eyes wide open, and it was quite late before they struck camp for the night. They made a fire and spread out their blankets and provisions.

While they ate darkness descended over the Ridge. The meal was a good one and the tired cadets ate heartily. Afterward they discussed the wisdom of keeping watch.

"Not that anyone will come along and gobble us up," said Terry, "but if that child should call out in the night we'd miss her if we were all asleep."

"That's true," Jim said. "And, anyway, I think we ought to have a fire going all night. We'll want one in the morning. That ghost is some human being bent on mischief and we must keep our eyes open for him. I'm sure he's mixed up in this thing, somehow."

This was agreed to and the boys figured out watches for themselves. During the evening, be fore they went to sleep, they sat around on their blankets and talked quietly, listening for any call or unusual sound. None came and at nine o'clock they decided to turn in.

* * * *

Throughout the night the separate watches were faithfully kept and the cadet who sat watch listened to the night sounds. But when the morning finally came and they rolled out at daybreak, not one of them had heard a single sound that would lead them to hope.

"We'll have to put in a good hard day," Don said, as they ate the last of their sandwiches.

Terry scrambled to his feet. "I'm going down to the brook and fill my canteen," he announced. "I don't know where there is a spring around and that brook looks perfectly all right."

"Maybe you had better boil the water and make sure before you drink it," Vench suggested.

Terry went back into the bushes some fifty feet until he found a gurgling little brook. The water looked cool and refreshing as it bubbled around the stones, and the redhead bent down to fill his canteen. It was then that a sound reached him, a sound that caused him to straighten up.

"Now, did the brook make that sound?" he wondered.

But it came again and Terry hesitated no longer. With a single bound he hopped across the water and parted the bushes on the other side. There, in a tiny hollow like a cave, her feet wet and her clothing covered with mud, sat the little Carson girl, her eyes red with weeping and her face swollen from her contact with vines and branches. She stared in wild terror at Terry as he broke his way through the bushes, but as he spoke to her the look faded for one of glad recognition.

A trembling gladness filled the boy. With a smothered cry he jumped at the child, sweeping her in his arms and pressing her to him as though she had been his own.

"You blessed little mischief-maker!" He choked. "What are you doing out here?"

"The ghost, he chase me," wailed the child, beginning to tremble. "I go for my dolly and the ghost come after me. I want my mama."

"You're going to have your mama," promised Terry. "So that confounded ghost is at the bottom of it, is he?"

"Yes, he chase me," sighed the child. "You're the soldier that ate mama's pie."

"That's right," grinned Terry. "Come along, I'm going to take you home."

He gathered the little body in his arms, easily jumped the creek, and fairly flew back to the camp. The others were rolling up their bundles as he dashed up.

"Took you a long time to get that water," Jim hailed.

"I'll show you what kind of water I got," whooped the happy redhead. "Allow me to introduce Miss Dorothy Carson!"

A medley of cries greeted the good news and the child and Terry were nearly knocked over in the rush. Dorothy Carson was pawed by the boys but did not seem to mind it.

"Where'd you find her?" Don asked, squeezing Terry's arm.

"Heard her crying back of some bushes," was the reply. "That darned old ghost chased her away from the house."

The return journey was swiftly made to Carson's house and the mother was nearly frantic with joy. At the farmhouse they found the colonel with Major Rhodes, and together they all listened to the story of the child regarding the ghost. She had gone out to get the doll, had seen the fearful shape near the chicken house, and too terrified to call out she had run away into the hills, where she had wandered until Terry had found her.

The boys were overwhelmed with thanks and praises and Terry's face became as red as his hair. The boastful sheriff was away at the time with a posse and there was no one to resent their success. After a happy time at the house they all went back to camp. Terry had the honor of firing the "Gossip" three times as the recall. Before two o'clock the entire corps was back in camp, eagerly e"changing news. All of them had searched faithfully.

Just before taps that night Jordan, Terry, Don, Jim, Douglas and Vench were requested to report to the colonel after drill on the following day. Wondering what could be in the wind the cadets went to bed, to sleep soundly after their strenuous search.

# CHAPTER 11

## THE GHOST PATROL

On the following day, when the General Orders were read, the cadets who had been most active in the search for Dorothy were warmly commended. All of the cadets were thanked by the colonel. Then the officers called for three rousing cheers for Cadet Mackson. These were given with a will.

"Mackson again!" hissed Cadet Rowen, under his breath. "It was only an accident and yet he gets a cheer for it. Wouldn't that make you sick?"

No one being addressed, no answer was given. But Terry himself felt that it was simply an accident.

"I just happened to be there at the brook at the right moment and heard her crying," he told his friends. "If I hadn't been the one, someone else would have run across her eventually. So I don't see what the fuss is all about."

"We make a fuss because you are such an old souse!" Jim laughed. "If you hadn't gone for a drink it might have been days before the child was found. Lucky thing you like to drink so much."

"I'll drink nothing but water all my life, in honor of the piece of service that drink did me," promised the redhead.

In the mess tent that noontime the colonel rapped on the head table for order. The rattling of spoons and plates became still and the cadets faced him expectantly.

"Gentlemen," said the colonel. "Since we have been here on the Ridge we have been quite deeply annoyed by this silly ghost that has been playing tricks in the neighborhood. I say silly in the sense that it is silly to play at such small things, but in another sense it may turn out to be something serious. I think that we have all had enough of the business and I promise you that if that ghost comes around the camp we will make short work of him. Now, what I want you to do is this: if you, any of you, learn anything definite about this ghost, either from hearsay or your own observations, I want all facts reported to me at once. Although we haven't time to go meddling all over the Ridge I think we are duty-bound to lay this ghost if possible, and so let me know whatever you learn about this ghost business."

There was a buzz as the headmaster sat down and the ghost of the Ridge furnished the topic for discussion during the rest of the meal. Drill ended that, and after the afternoon work was over the cadets named on the previous evening reported at the colonel's big tent. He was waiting for them.

"Sit down anywhere you can, boys," he told them. "On the bed or the chairs. I guess we can find room for all of us. Will you pull the flap closed, Captain Jordan?"

Jordan obeyed and the colonel faced his interested boys. "Well, you heard what I had to say today at the mess tent regarding the responsibility of each cadet in regard to the ghost trouble on this Ridge. That will do very nicely for the corps at large, for if I gave some of them too much authority some grave mistakes of over-zealousness would probably follow. But to you young men I want to give a commission that I'm sure you will handle with care and tact."

He paused and nothing was said. Crossing his knees the colonel went on: "I spoke of the fact that ruining this ghost and his game was our duty as citizens, and it is. Inquiry has revealed that the people hereabouts are very superstitious, and they have taken this ghost on trust for several years. Of course, in a community of sensible men and women the thing would have been run out long ago, but there is just enough fear and superstition in the people around here to imagine this ghost to be the real thing and not some human being who is simply playing on their fears and ignorance. You may have noticed that when we brought that child back to Mrs. Carson she simply said: 'I'll never let you out again where that ghost can scare you.' No question or thought about driving him away, but just a passive resignation to the fact that he is here and belongs here.

"But this ghost does not belong here, boys, and we must see to it that he does not stay here. At school we teach you that every man has a duty to the public, and even here, in a strange country, we have our challenge. We must track down this ghost and expose him. We have the right to do so because he has invaded our camp and stampeded our horses. But I want the whole thing done quietly and steady heads must take up the task. I have therefore picked you young men to tackle this problem."

"I'm sure we'll enjoy it, sir!" smiled Jordan.

"What I want you to do is this," nodded the colonel. "I want you six cadets to form yourself into a secret Ghost Patrol. You are to keep it strictly to yourselves, and you are to make every effort to get some trace of this ghost. I give you full liberty to leave camp at any hour, and every hour, to pass sentries whenever it is really necessary, and to cut drill if the necessity should arise. I am not going to tell you how you should go about it, because I really don't know myself, but I will leave the working out of plans to you. Obviously, it will be out of the question to simply rove over the Ridge in a band, for that would soon advertise itself, but I'm sure you will make a plan that will bring results. If at any time there is a call that the ghost has been sighted around the camp you will dash out and make a thorough search for him. I guess that is all clear, isn't it?"

"I think so, sir," replied Jordan. "We'll do the best that we can for the community in this case. I have heard that in the last few years a number of good, honest families have left the Ridge simply because of this silly situation, and a thing like that has no business to be."

"You're right, it has no business to be," retorted the colonel. "Not when an individual rolls a blazing hay wagon downhill and burns up a man's barn, and then scares a child away from her home. To say nothing of stampeding our horses."

"What do you think of that theory regarding the Maul and Hyde feud, colonel?" Don asked, from his seat on the cot.

"I think there may be something in it," was the answer. "I can't find out what the feud was all about, and probably the present families don't know, so stupid are such things. It is much like those you hear about in the Kentucky mountains, where families kill each other off for generations over causes that never touched them personally. But I gather that the last of the Mauls was supposed to have been drowned and his body was never found. That points to only one thing."

"You think that he is alive and doing all this ghost business?" Jim asked.

"I wouldn't be surprised. As far as I can learn no one but the Hydes have ever been actively molested. Numbers of persons have been scared by the sight of the white shape, but only the Hydes have been harmed. If it had not been for the heroic work done by you cadets the other night Hyde would have been burned completely out of house and home."

"Now that every sentry has been told to promptly report any trace of the ghost we may have an even chance of nailing him," Douglas observed.

"Yes, though you may have to work fast. Well, that will be all. You will kindly keep that to yourselves and consider yourselves as a special Ghost Patrol."

When they had left the colonel the cadets separated and went to their tents. While preparing for the evening meal they talked things over.

"If you notice, the colonel spoke about the ghost starting the stampede," Jim said, as he washed vigorously. "That shows that he believes my story."

"I guess there is no doubt of that," responded Don. "He simply can't doubt Rowen's word on the face of it."

Before the evening meal was ready it began to rain. The cadets had been fortunate in the weather during their stay in camp, and up to the present time only showers had occurred occasionally. But tonight the rain meant business, for it settled in for a long spell. Before long the company streets were a mass of mud. It was necessary to make a dash for the mess tent, and all the time they ate the steady pouring of the rain could be heard on the canvas overhead.

There were no campfires that night and the cadets clustered in their own tents. The sentries looked forward to a bleak and joyless patrol, but the colonel knew that a sample of army life under all conditions was good for the young soldiers. As long as they were well-shod and amply protected from the rain there was no danger of sickness, and a taste of duty under stern circumstances was beneficial rather than harmful to the cadets.

Jordan, Vench and Douglas slopped their way over to the tent occupied by the three friends. This tent was the end one on the rear company street, backed up against the woods. The tent light made the place seem homelike, and it was warm inside.

"Fine night, if anyone likes it," grinned Vench, as he took off his wet raincoat. "We didn't have anything else to do so we came over."

"Glad to have you," smiled Don. "It looks like a particularly dull evening. I'll bet we'll harp on the one subject, though."

"On the glories of the Ghost Patrol, eh?" laughed Jordan.

"How did you guess?" Don retorted.

"This is something new," Douglas said. "Early in the year the Mercers, Terry and I were on the beach patrol, but this is the first time I ever heard of a Ghost Patrol."

"All I hope is that we get some results out of this new organization," Terry said.

They talked of the task ahead of them for some time. Suddenly Jim held up his hand, signaling for silence.

"Did you fellows hear anything?" he asked.

No one had. "What was it like?" Jordan asked.

"I thought I heard someone close to the back of the tent," said Jim, slipping on his raincoat. "Wait'll I take a look."

"Who would sneak around a tent on a night like this?" scoffed Vench, as Jim slipped out.

"Didn't see anything," Jim said, returning and shaking the rain off his coat.

"We hope you don't hear anything else tonight," grumbled Terry. "Might as well bring a dog in here to shake himself!"

Long before taps the visitors had gone and the friends turned in. In the morning the rain had stopped, but a gray sky hung over the camp. Just as assembly was breaking up the Officer on Inspection reported to the colonel.

"Something to show you on a tree at the end of the camp, sir," he reported.

The cadets swarmed around the colonel as he took a heavy piece of cardboard from a tree not far from the tent occupied by the Mercers and Terry. In large, crude letters this warning was written:

**YOU DURNED TIN SOLDIERS KEEP YOURE NOSE OUTN THE GHOST BUSINESS.**

# CHAPTER 12

## A BRUSH WITH THE SHERIFF

THE cardboard had been propped up in the space provided by a small branch. The letters had been wet and faint streaks showed where they had run.

"The sentries who were on duty last night please step forward," requested the colonel. A number of cadets promptly stepped forward, facing the colonel.

"Did any one of you at any time during the night see or hear anyone around the camp?" Not one sentry had noted anything amiss.

"I can tell you of an experience that happened to us last night, colonel," spoke up Jim. "We were discussing the whole ghost situation on the Ridge, and our determination to find out who this ghost was, when we heard a noise outside our tent. I might more accurately say that I heard it, and I went outside to see if anyone was there. I didn't find anyone, but it looks as though someone did sneak up to our tent, hear what we had to say, and then printed this sign to scare us."

"But in order to do so the party must have gone back to some shelter and spent some time making up the warning, if such it might be called," mused the headmaster. "I have no doubt, however, that your conversation was overheard. This ghost has developed a bad habit of visiting our camp whenever he feels like it."

"It wouldn't have been hard to slip past a sentry in the pouring rain, sir," suggested Jordan.

"No, not at all," agreed the colonel. "With this reference to your soldiering, I presume that you young men will have an added cause now to go after this ghost person."

"That's a pretty heavy insult!" Major Rhodes smiled.

"Well, the ghost must know now that an active campaign is afoot to drive him off the Ridge," said the colonel. "That ought to make the game more interesting than ever. Our foe is warned and will play his game with skill. That gives you boys greater odds to move against, but I feel sure that you will be successful in making an end to the affair."

The regular routine of that day seemed to take longer than usual, but as soon as it was over the members of the Ghost Patrol gathered together to look around in back of the camp for signs of the night visitor. The ground was wet and they argued that if the prowler ever left any traces he would surely have done so that night. Their first search took in the soft soil back of Jim's tent and they found encouraging signs at once.

"More than one footprint here," proclaimed Don, grimly, as they bent over the depressions in the dirt.

Someone had sneaked up close to the wall of the tent, and the prints of large shoes were very plain. In the heels of the left shoe they found a peculiarity that gave them something to work on. There had been some kind of a cut down the center of the leather heel and it showed plainly in the soft mud.

"Maybe when the heel was cut out of block leather the knife slipped and left that mark," Jordan thought. "With a plain marking like that we ought not to have much trouble. Let's look under that tree where the cardboard was found."

Under this tree they had more difficulty, because the feet of the curious cadets had churned up the ground so that it was almost impossible to make out anything definite. But at a distance of perhaps three yards they found the marked heel print again. Whoever had placed the sign in the tree had come down the slope above the camp, and the print could be followed for a short distance up the hillside. But before long they struck a section of rocky ground and hunt as they would they could not find another trace of the print.

"A whole lot of this Ridge is pretty rocky," sighed Douglas. "From here on I guess we'll have to trust to luck. Somewhere we may run across the trail again and get our bearings."

They explored the slope with exhausting patience, but there was no further trace until they struck the very top of the hill. There, in a soft spot, they once more found their marking. The print pointed down toward the town of Rideway, which they could see in the distance.

"He went down into town," said Terry. "Suppose we follow down there, and see where the print leads to?"

Following the marked heel down into Rideway was not an easy task. In some places they lost all traces of it and had to look around for half an hour before finding the faint mark again. But the trail led steadily down the opposite slope from the camp until it went into town. But here they lost it for good.

The main road was hard as a rock, with a glazed surface that left no trace of any mark. They followed this road down through town for a long way, but there was no further sign of the marked heel. Their next move was to look along the sides of the road to see if the man had walked off it at any point, but after a good hour had been spent in this way the cadets gave it up as a bad job.

"Too bad," groaned Jim. "Right at the most important part we lose it altogether. I guess that's the end of an important clue."

"Yes, looks like we have exhausted this possibility," agreed Jordan. "Anyway, we have given the town people something to wonder about." This was true. The natives of Rideway had been watching the boys with curiosity. So busy had they been in their search that they had failed to pay any attention to the citizens, but the people had not failed to note what they were doing.

"Say," Don warned. "Here comes that nasty sheriff."

From a small, one-story shack near them the tall sheriff made his way. His eyes were fixed on the boys and he swaggered in their direction. They were not aware of it, but he had been watching them from his window for the last several minutes.

"Let's be careful what we say to this fellow," Terry warned in a low voice. "We'll tell him we just came to town for a visit."

The sheriff had now come within hailing distance. Hands on hips he surveyed the cadets with vast contempt.

"What're you soldier boys doing here?" he boomed in a voice sufficiently loud to attract the attention of the passers-by. A small ring instantly collected.

"We're just looking your town over," smiled Jordan easily.

"Looking my town over, eh? I guess you are pretty thorough about it. Examining the streets to see what kind of dust we have here, I see."

"Yes," nodded Terry innocently. "It is just like the dust they have every place else!"

"You keep your mouth closed, young fellow!" rumbled the sheriff, turning smoldering eyes on the cheerful redhead. "If I have any funny talk from you boys I'll lock you up quicker'n a wink. I want to know what you boys are doing snooping around the street here."

"We're here looking for a man who has been prowling about our camp lately," said Jordan, seeing that nothing was to be gained by evading the issue any longer.

"What man is prowling around your camp?" the sheriff demanded.

"That's just what we would like to know," responded the senior captain. "Not long ago a man stampeded our horses and last night he left a warning in our tree in our camp, telling us to keep our noses out of this ghost business. We found a heel print in the mud under that tree and we have followed it down into this town. That's all."

"Nobody has been anywhere near your camp," the sheriff declared loudly. "You boys have been dreaming."

"Is that so?" spoke up Jim, sharply. "Listen here, Mr. Sheriff, I saw that man stampede our horses. Whoever is hanging around the camp had better keep away from it and stay away."

"What'll you do if he doesn't stay away?" scoffed the sheriff.

"We'll do what you should have done long ago," snapped Don. "We'll find him and send him to a responsible officer of the law to take care of. You are supposed to be a sheriff here, keeping law and order, and yet a silly ghost terrifies the community for years and you aren't able to run him down. We're neither too stupid nor too lazy to do it and if the ghost or any of his friends are here in this crowd I'm telling you plainly that we're going to nail him and nail him hard!"

There was an awed rustle in the crowd. The sheriff turned purple with wrath. He shook a long and bony finger at the cadets.

"You imitation soldiers, listen to me," he roared. "I'm warning you to keep your nose out of affairs on this Ridge! I'm the sheriff here and what I say goes. If I catch you meddling around with anything again I'll lock you up so fast you won't know what hit you. You mind your own business about people and things at Rustling Ridge, do you get me?"

"As far as people on the Ridge go, we do get you," retorted Jordan. "But not where it concerns this ghost who has been coming into our camp at night. If he insists upon visiting us, then it is our business to try to find him. That's all there is to that."

Realizing that there was no use in arguing further the boys left.

"Well, that's an open declaration of war," chuckled Terry, as they made their way back to camp. "I'm afraid we'll have to buck that sheriff all the way along the line."

"Yes, because it is even possible that he has something to do with the ghost business himself," said Vench, seriously. "Anyway, he is mighty touchy about the whole thing."

"That is because he considers himself the King of the Ridge, and it hurts his pride to see anyone else butt in," said Jim. "Wonder what the colonel will say when we tell him?"

The colonel heard them in silence. Then he spoke to them quietly. "You did perfectly right, boys," he said. "However, in the future steer clear of him. I don't think he really amounts to much, but he may make things pretty unpleasant. In spite of him, we'll get this ghost yet."

The colonel accompanied the boys to the tent entrance when they left. Outside they found Lieutenant Thompson with a number of other cadets staring fixedly across the Ridge.

At the sound of the colonel's voice Thompson turned his gaze to the headmaster and said, "Sir, I believe that someone is sending us a wigwag message from that hill!"

All eyes swung toward the distant hill. Sure enough, far up at the top two tiny white flags moved in the semaphore signal. Whoever was doing it knew the code and they stared in fascination as the flags moved steadily.

"He is repeating his message, boys," said the colonel, breaking the silence that had settled upon them. "Be sure you get it this time."

The camp was completely silent as the cadets strained their eyes to read the wigwag message. When it finished a burst of excitement and amazement followed. The mysterious flagman had signaled unmistakably: "Be on your guard. The Ghost walks tonight!"

# CHAPTER 13

## THE SHAPE IN THE MOONLIGHT

Great was the astonishment as the cadets made out the signal from the opposite side of the hill. At least nine-tenths of them had read the message accurately, for a knowledge of signaling, both in the Morse code and the semaphore, was required at the school. After the message was received they stood staring toward the hill, looking for some further word. When the same message had been repeated three times the colonel awoke to the fact that the signalman was not going to say anything more.

"Mr. Walker," he called to the best signalman that the corps had. "Get your flags and answer 'All right.'"

Cadet Walker departed on a run to his tent, to reappear shortly with two white flags. Standing where he would surely be seen by the lone signalman, the cadet began his message. The flags on the other side of the Ridge disappeared at once as the man read their signal, and Walker stopped his rapid arm movements.

"Now, what in the world do you make of that?" Terry asked, in amazement. His question was taken up by all of the cadets and asked without any satisfactory answer. Supper was neglected while the mystery was considered, and the colonel was as much puzzled as the boys were.

When the cadets finally did sit down to supper the tables buzzed with speculative talk. Many were for going over to that hill and finding out who it could have been that signaled them. At the close of the meal the colonel rapped for order and when the tent had become quiet he spoke to them of the future plans.

"I know as little about that signal as you do, boys," he said, "but I believe it to be sincere. Someone who is friendly is trying to give us a warning that may stand us in good stead. It is also possible that it may be a hoax, simply designed to fool us or to draw us out of camp. That will not happen, you may be sure, but I feel that we should be ready for duty. I shall split the battalion in half, and one-half of you will patrol the Ridge while the other half remains in camp to guard it against surprise."

There was a stirring and a ripple of genuine pleasure at the news, for all of the young men looked forward to some exciting times ahead. Each one was wishing that he would be lucky enough to be in the group that would patrol the Ridge.

"I wish to make this statement, which is also an order," went on the colonel. "There will be no carrying of arms tonight. Some one of you might become excited and fire at the wrong time, so I expressly forbid it. It is not as though you were going out alone, but you are going out in groups and therefore a weapon, in the shape of a firearm, won't be necessary. I trust that five or six husky young cadets will be a match for the best ghost this Ridge can send against us. It may be that we will have our supreme chance to end this ugly ghost business tonight, and if so I want no slips that will damage the prospect. I wish to see the leaders immediately after the meal."

When the colonel met with the leaders he specified which cadets were to go out and which ones were to stay at camp. To their joy all of the friends of Don and Jim were to patrol the Ridge. The colonel had suggested that the Ghost Patrol go in a body, so the members of that secret organization prepared to go out alone. The leaders passed from group to group, telling them where to go and how to act, signals were arranged, and the stage was set.

To the waiting cadets it seemed that evening ~was unusually slow in coming. No attempt was made to slip out of camp until full darkness had come, for if anyone was watching it would be a risky thing to do.

"Never saw a day last so long in my life," grumbled Vench, digging his heel into the soft mud.

"It is just about the usual length, I guess," smiled Don. "One thing is going to be for and against us tonight."

"What is that?" the others asked.

"There will be just enough of a moon to make us have to be careful, and just enough to help us spot the ghost if he gets out into the open."

Jordan emerged from his tent and stopped at the various groups to give some sort of an order. When he got to the members of the Ghost Patrol he repeated it finally.

"When we leave the camp we are to leave by the back way, taking care to keep out of the light of the fires," he told them. "It is possible that someone is watching the camp and our game would be spoiled if we walked out in such a way that it could be seen. In about a half hour we will be able to get going."

"The bunch in camp will have to keep their eyes wide open," said Douglas.

"Yes, and the colonel will be helping them do it. We have to be careful that this isn't all some tricky plan to pull us out of camp while somebody with kindly ideas rushes in and burns the place out. The colonel has arranged this signal: three rifle shots for a recall. That will mean trouble in the camp, and if you hear it, head for camp as fast as you can go."

Darkness finally fell and the stars appeared faintly in the summer sky as the slice of the moon cut the distant horizon.

One group broke up and disappeared back of the tents and another followed. Jordan got up.

"All right, let's go," he announced, glancing at his watch. "Slip out of camp without a sound. Keep to the shadows."

The group in the tent broke up at once, some of them walking down the company street for a distance of three or four tents and then slipping behind them. Once out of the glare of the several campfires they had no trouble in gaining the shelter of the trees, and after a few seconds they were all together.

"Which direction now?" Jim asked.

"Let's go clear to the top of the Ridge," suggested Jordan. "From there we can get a comprehensive view of the woods and hills and spot anything that moves."

They set out for the top of the Ridge, walking with care and listening for every sound that might break the stillness. They had not gone far before there was a noise as though someone was moving before them. Spreading out fanwise they bore silently down on the spot from which the noise had come only to run into another patrol which was lying low and waiting for them to come forward.

"Oh, it is only you guys," grunted Jordan, as Cadets Perry, Noxan, Dodge and Orlan confronted them.

"Yes, sorry to disappoint you by not being the ghost!" Perry grinned. "But we heard you coming along and we took to cover, so that you would run into us. I'm afraid that we'll be doing that all evening."

"Well, then let's get over it by giving the school whistle every time," suggested Don. "If we had whistled then you would have replied and we would have passed you in another direction."

"A good idea, Mercer," approved Dodge. "If we give the whistle and fail to receive the answer, we'll know that the party before us is a suspicious case. We can then go after them in earnest."

"Yes, that will be OK," nodded the senior captain. "We are striking off here, boys. See you later."

With that they left the party and continued their journey to the top of the hill. From there they could look all along the Ridge, and even see the faint gleam of their own campfires in the distance. There was no sign of life on the Ridge,, but that was inconclusive, for they knew that directly below them several bands of cadets were moving around.

"For the time being at least we will just stay here and sweep the hills with our eyes," Jordan said.

For a full hour they sat under a tree, well-sheltered in its shadows, and looked searchingly at the slopes below them. In that time the only life they saw were the forms of several cadets who appeared briefly in the open and then were lost in the darkness. Finally they became highly impatient at the inaction.

"I guess there is nothing to be gained by sitting here," Jordan said. "My suggestion is that we split up and move along the top of the Ridge in opposite directions. Suppose Terry, Jim and Don come with me, and Thompson, Douglas and Vench group together and go toward the east of the Ridge? We'll work back past the camp."

"Sounds as good as anything," nodded Thompson. "Most of our cadets are content to stay down on the slopes, so it wouldn't be a bad idea to keep to the top."

"Yes, and here's another thing," put in Terry. "You three are going toward the town. Why not keep an eye on that side of the Ridge and see if this ghost doesn't come up from town, if he comes at all."

"There may be something in that," said Jordan. "We'll watch this side of the hill. By the way, have all of you fellows got your cadet whistles?"

All of them had the regular whistles, similar to those used by traffic policemen. "If you get into a scrape and need help, just blow like mad," commanded Jordan. "If we should run into anything we'll do the same."

With this word they separated. They were now so high above the camp that the fires gleamed like little fireflies below them.

"Somebody or something moving in the bushes below!" whispered Jim, suddenly. He pointed into a small gully below them and they looked down. The bushes, clearly seen in the pale moonlight, were moving.

"I'll whistle," said Jordan, and did so. But there was no reply.

"Down we go, and see who it is," decided the captain, and they crept forward stealthily, careful to make as little noise as possible. But when they dipped down in the gully they found four cadets, one of whom was Rowen. These cadets were standing like statues, evidently a bit scared and waiting to see who it was that moved toward them.

"Didn't you fellows hear my whistle?" Jordan demanded.

"We thought we heard someone whistle," replied Cadet Motley. "But we weren't sure."

"Well, I whistled," Jordan said. "Whenever you hear that you'll know that friends are near by." Jordan then repeated Don's suggestion to use their special whistle for recognizing cadets.

"OK," nodded Motley. "What time have you, Jordan? I'm not sure about my watch."

Jordan drew out his watch. "I have just eleven o'clock, Motley," he replied. "I guess—"

Jim gripped his arm. "Siss—s!" he hissed. "Look, on the top of the Ridge!"

With one accord they looked up the slope and their blood chilled. In a patch of moonlight a weird and terrible figure walked swiftly from one patch of darkness toward another. It looked to be the figure of a man, clothed entirely in white. It glanced neither to the right nor to the left, but strode swiftly along, to all intents and purposes unaware that anyone save itself was on the Ridge. Even the head was muffled in white and showed no trace of eyes, nose or mouth. Quiet and evil and sinister did it look as it glided past the dark background of the sky.

# CHAPTER 14

## DISOBEDIENCE LOSES THE GAME

THE cadets instinctively crouched down where they stood. It seemed to be the proper thing to do, although the ghostly figure had not looked in their direction.

The moment was one of indecision. While the ghost kept in plain sight on the top of the Ridge they were content to watch it, waiting for a cue that would send them into action. To attempt to rush up the hill and grapple with the shape would be the wrong thing to do, for the noise of their approach would startle the thing into a run. To trail it as quietly as possible was their only thought.

There was a stir on the part of one of the cadets, the one nearest Don. He reached into his inside pocket and then brought his hand out into the open. It was Dick Rowen who had moved and Don shifted his eyes toward him.

What he saw startled him. Against all orders to the contrary the sulky cadet had brought a revolver with him. He was even now raising it and pointing toward the white shape.

Don's arm described a sort of arc, his hand coming down with a thump on the wrist of the unpopular cadet. But Rowen had a good grip on the stock of his revolver.

"Put that away, Rowen," Don whispered, sternly.

"Leave me alone, Mercer," hissed the other. "I'm just going to scare the thing."

Don's grasp tightened and he jerked the wrist toward him. Rowen promptly twisted his arm, pointing the revolver upward. The grasp of his fingers on the trigger was too strong and the revolver went off with a shattering report.

There was a moment of utter silence from the boys themselves. The figure in white leaped into the air and then began a swift run along the top of the Ridge. Don had dropped Rowen's wrist in dismay and the other cadet was shaken by the unexpected happening.

"Oh, you stupid guy!" cried Don, as the ghost could be heard running along the rise.

They were all on their feet now and Jordan pushed up to them. He grasped the cadet by the arm.

"Rowen, what in the world did you do that for?" he ground out.

"I didn't do it," defended the other. "Mercer grabbed my arm."

"Never mind the excuses, we all saw what you did. It was against the colonel's orders to carry any kind of a gun. Why did—"

Don cut in. "Some of you fellows get after the ghost on the double!" he cried, and Terry, Jim, and the others ran off, leaving him alone with Jordan and the angry one.

"Well, I thought the colonel was foolish about not carrying arms," said Rowen, as the others breasted the rise. "Anyway, what right had he to send us out to face some kind of a desperate man, maybe a criminal, without any way to protect ourselves? I wasn't going to shoot the man, I was going to scare him."

"You succeeded in doing that without carrying out your original plan," Jordan returned, grimly. "Now, Rowen, I want you to march yourself back to camp and put yourself on report. You are under arrest."

"Oh, sure, I could expect that from you!" said Rowen, bitterly.

"Yes, you could, you or anyone else who had pulled a stunt like that," nodded Jordan. "It was direct and defiant disobedience, and if we lose our chance to nab the ghost it will be entirely your fault. Return to camp at once, Rowen."

"OK," grumbled Rowen. He walked sullenly away.

"Now, if we are going to catch up with the boys we'll have to put all we have into it," announced Jordan.

"Right!" said Don, as they started up the slope. "Feel equal to a good stiff run?"

"Sure," smiled Jordan. "Let's hit a steady pace."

Gaining the top of the rise they fell into a steady run along the top, away from the camp and toward the town on the far side of the Ridge. They were following a general direction, which was not entirely blind, for far ahead of them they heard a faint cracking sound that seemed to be made by someone running recklessly. Their route did not keep them long on the top of the hill, for the ghost had taken to the deeper shelter of the trees lower down and they plunged down the slope, threading their way in between the trees.

They almost fell over a figure that was before them in the woods. It was Cadet Owens, and he was sitting on a rock, hugging his foot. His shoe was off and he was breathing hard.

"Hurt yourself?" Jordan called.

"Not much," gasped Owens. "Got my shoe caught in a piece of rock and twisted my ankle. But I'll be able to walk. Keep on going straight ahead. We didn't lose sight of him."

The other two plunged on, following a straight line. They did not expect to overtake the others, for Terry and Jim in particular were fast runners and they had had a good start. All they could hope to do was to be in at the finish if there was a finish, and with this in mind they ran on.

"Rough going!" gasped Don, as they began to ascend a second rolling hill.

"Nothing else but!" said Jordan, running steadily.

On the top of the hill they found themselves in familiar country. Far ahead of them was the tiny cabin of Peter Vancouver and above them was the big, barn-like house that they had observed at the time they first took the hike to the old man's place. N ow they were somewhat at a loss, and slowed up a bit in their running.

"We'll have to be careful not to lose them now," Don said.

"There they are, right ahead of us," announced Jordan. "They must have lost him, because they are just standing there."

"They are right in front of that old house," observed Don, as they ran forward.

The others turned in glad surprise when the two ran up.

"Did you lose him?" Jordan called, as they joined them.

"He just bolted into that house," Terry answered. "Think we ought to go in after him?"

"Absolutely," was the reply from the senior captain. "All you fellows have your flashlights, haven't you?"

They all had. Jordan led the way inside the gate and they walked with great care toward the house.

"He was way ahead of us," said Motley, "and just as soon as he got to this old house he bolted right inside. He may be armed, so we had better be careful."

"Yes," replied Jordan. "But if he is in the house we are bound to get him. Be ready to put your light out if he tries any shooting. And be careful of holes or anything in the house."

They snapped on their flashlights as they went up the tottering old porch of what had once been a fine old mansion. There were no windows in the place which could boast of glass, and the front door had dropped from its hinges and now lay sprawled out on the porch. Jordan swung his light down on this prostrate door, and they could see that it was covered with dirt and mud. Newer marks on the door showed that someone had recently entered the place.

"This is where he went, all right," said Don. "On your toes, everybody."

Before entering the place they flashed brilliant beams of light in every corner of the nearest room. This was a large hall, with bare walls from which the plaster had fallen, and a large staircase running up to a second floor. Realizing that the ghost might leave the place by some rear door while they prowled around the front rooms, the cadets pushed the search with all possible speed, their eyes and ears alert for any sign of someone lurking. But a rapid search of a wide parlor, a square dining room, and an enormous kitchen showed them that at least no one was concealed downstairs.

"I guess our next move will be the upstairs," Motley suggested, and they took the wide steps toward the top of the house.

Here there were a number of smaller rooms and it took them some little time to look through all of them. Nothing was to be found on the second floor, and with more confidence they went to the third floor. This was a big barn-like attic, and was obviously quite empty.

"Well, if he is in the place at all, it is the cellar," decided Jordan, when they had satisfied themselves that there was no one in the upper part of the house. "I don't think he came upstairs at all, because I don't see any prints."

There were some footprints in the lower hall but they were lost on the comparatively bare stretches of floor. The cellar, which extended only a short distance under the house, was tenanted by spiders only, and no one had been in there, judging by the huge webs that stretched across the bottom of the stairway. It would have been impossible for anyone to have gone that way without breaking the webs, and they were all intact.

"Many thanks to the spiders," acknowledged Terry, lifting his hat. "They make it possible for us to keep from going any deeper into this damp hole. The smell of it is enough for me."

"Just to make doubly sure," said Jordan, "suppose we go around to the back and see if there is an outside cellar door? The ghost may have run out the back door of the house and down a back stairs to the cellar. I'm not going to give up the search until I have seen every corner of the house."

"While a couple of us are doing that I suggest that two or three of us look in the closets on the first floor," Don advanced. "We missed them on our first round. I guess a couple of us can hold the ghost in a tussle until the others get on the spot."

"All right," said Jordan. "Jim and Motley, come with me. The rest of you scatter. But I'm pretty sure that the ghost ran right on through the house and escaped into the woods."

The others thought the same thing, but they scattered to search. Terry and Cadet Ross began to look into the closets on the first floor. Don wandered back into the parlor and came to the front porch. From there he looked off over the hills, seeing below him the lights in Vancouver's cabin.

"I wonder if old Mr. Vancouver is all right?" Don mused. "Maybe he heard the noise we made and is alarmed. It isn't far to his house, and I think I'll run down and see if he is all right. Won't take a second, and I'll be right back."

# CHAPTER 15

## DAWNING LIGHT

With this kindly thought in mind Don jumped to the ground and started off. But at that moment Terry appeared in the black doorway.

"Hey, where are you going?" the redhead asked. "Just going to run down and see if Mr. Vancouver is OK," called back Don. "Tell Jordan that I'll be right back."

"All right, kid," Terry returned. "If you run into any trouble, just sing out and we'll come on the double."

Terry turned back and was lost to sight while Don resumed his journey down the slope. The cabin was not far away and it took him but a moment to reach it. He approached it from the back, hoping to get a look in one of the windows, but they were too high and small in the rear and so he passed around to the front of the cabin. Noiselessly he crossed the porch and tapped on the door, waiting for an answer.

Although he waited there was no response and he wondered if the old man was asleep. Since there was a light showing he rather doubted that and he knocked again, a trifle louder. The light came out from under the door and showed around the windows that opened off the porch, but he was unable to peer in because heavy black shades were pulled down to the bottom. The front door was solid and he found no help in that direction.

"He must be asleep, in spite of the light," Don decided. "I'll see if I can see anything through the side windows."

He made his way around the side of the house and found that he could see in a window there. A ragged shade had been pulled down but the torn edges gave him a limited view of the interior of the large room. It was lighted by a single oil lamp, and in a far corner sat the invalid in his chair, apparently fast asleep. At least he was very quiet and Don was undecided.

"Don't know as I ought to tap, but I'll just see if he is awake," he decided, and tapped with his ring on the glass in the window. The old man stirred, looked toward the window, and wheeled his chair out of the shadow.

"Who is it?" he cried, in a shrill voice.

Don ran swiftly around the porch and placed his lips near the door frame. "It is Don Mercer, one of the cadets who visited you one afternoon," he called. "May I come in?"

"Sure, you may," responded the man, instantly. There was a soft sound, like the rolling of wheels, and the catch on the door rattled. In an instant the door swung open to show the frail figure in the chair. Don was bathed in a yellow light that blinded him for a moment.

"Come right in," invited Vancouver, spinning back from the door. "Close the door and make yourself right at home. What brings you up here at this hour?"

Don entered, closing the door back of him, and looked around the room. A fire snapped in an open hearth and the room was a bit too warm. Vancouver was wrapped in a brown blanket, and he had wheeled himself back into the shadows beyond the lamp light.

"I'll have to apologize for my late call, Mr. Vancouver," laughed Don. "But a bunch of us chased the ghost up this way and the rest of the boys are looking for him. I saw your lights down here and just ran in to see if you were all right, or if our noise had alarmed you."

"You were chasing the ghost!" cried Vancouver, sharply. "Go on!"

"Yes, we saw him walking along the Ridge and we gave chase," Don explained. "We trailed him into that old house on the top of the hill and we went all through the place but couldn't find him. While the others were looking I ran down here to see if you had heard anything. Sorry to have bothered you."

"Wasn't any bother at all, and I'm grateful to you for your thought," responded Vancouver promptly. "I didn't hear anything because I've been sleeping here in the chair. Your knock woke me up. So you saw the ghost, eh? What did he look like?"

Don described the appearance of the ghost and the old man appeared to be deeply interested.

"You say you fellows saw him. How'd you come to do that? You ain't always out of your camp so late as this, be you?"

Feeling that he might some day help them to find the ghost, Don related the story of the mysterious flagman, the search on the hill and the revolver shot that Rowen had fired off.

"Dear, too bad about that shot," said the invalid, shaking his head. "If it hadn't been for that you would have nailed this ghost, eh?"

"No doubt of it," said Don, his attention attracted by something that the man was doing. "Are you too hot, Mr. Vancouver?"

The invalid had been passing a hand jerkily across his forehead several times, and each time after the act he wiped a somewhat dampened hand on the brown cover. Although it was quite warm in the place it did not seem to be hot enough to make a man sweat, unless Mr. Vancouver was the kind who perspired easily. It seemed to Don that the old man was breathing pretty heavily for one who had sat in a wheel chair all evening, and in the boy's brain a faint idea stirred. He rejected it, at first, but like a gentle knocking it persisted.

"Oh, no, no," hastily interposed the cripple. "Do you feel too warm?"

"No, but I thought perhaps you might be a little hot, and I'd open a window or the door for you," responded Don, seating himself on the edge of the table.

"No, you needn't do that," said the man, running one thumb absently along the edge of the nearest wheel. The glance that he fixed on the cadet's face was keen and almost fierce. "I'm so old I got to keep warm, because I don't move around enough."

"I see," nodded Don. He had intended to leave immediately, but found himself suddenly possessed with a desire to remain. "Well, as I was telling you, we chased that ghost into the old house above you. Know anything about the place?"

At the same time Don began a rigid inspection of his host. Most of the man was covered up, but his feet showed under the blanket. Only the toes could be seen, but there was something about them that attracted his attention. They were clothed in socks which seemed to be damp, and he wondered if the man always went without shoes.

Vancouver knew the place well. "They used to call that the haunted house, around here," he chuckled. "This Ridge is a pretty spooky place, the more you hear of it. You don't know who it was that sent you that flag message, eh?"

"Haven't the least idea," answered Don. "All of the cadets were in camp at the time, and I don't know who around here knows how to use signal flags. And who would know that the ghost was going to walk?"

"You beat me there," Vancouver said, shaking his head. "That's a hard nut to crack. Maybe the ghost went in for a little advertising."

"I doubt it, Mr. Vancouver," said Don, noting that the fire was consuming fresh wood which couldn't have been put there an hour ago. "If you had seen the ghost run you'd have known that the thing was utterly unexpected to him. It is a pretty tough problem."

"I guess most ghost doings are tough problems," grinned the old man.

"I guess so," Don smiled. "Nice fire you have there. We don't see many open hearth fires any more. Have you had it going all evening?"

"Yep, I generally have it going every evening," responded the man, somewhat absently.

"Well, I'll have to be running along, Mr. Vancouver," he said, glancing at his watch. "I don't want to keep you at an hour like this. I just wanted to run down and see if we had alarmed you, but as long as we haven't, why, I'll be moving."

"I didn't hear a sound, so I'm all right. It was real nice of you to drop down to see if I was all right, and I sure appreciate that. An old cripple like me doesn't get much chance to see the world or talk with anyone, so it did me good to have you stop in."

"That's fine," replied Don, his eyes busy at the task of looking around the room in a guarded manner. "Say, Mr. Vancouver, as I told you before, we did quite a bit of running tonight. And gee, I'm just about burning up with thirst. I'm thinking with pleasure that you have some of the finest water I ever tasted here."

"I'll get you a drink in just a shake," promised the man, seizing his wheel.

"Don't bother. Can't I get it myself?" asked Don, wishing to gain a look at the kitchen.

"Won't take me a second," said the other, and spun around in his chair, aiming at the doorway that led into the back room. With the speed and accuracy of an arrow he passed through it and was gone.

And almost immediately Don thanked his lucky stars that he had not been permitted to go out into the other room himself. For something that had been hidden by the chair of the cripple was now disclosed. In the corner rested a pair of shoes, and these shoes were covered with mud!

Not the slightest doubt about it. Red and black mud, soft and wet, a fact that he could determine without touching them. A band of light from the lamp shone on them and revealed the evidence plainly. That explained the man's damp socks. Yet Don's brain was unable to fully take it all in.

"Is it possible that this man is not an invalid after all? Or has the real ghost been here, and maybe is hiding here right now? That may be possible."

But certain things pointed an unerring hand at his host. His brow was moist, as of one who had been running. His breath had been rapid, and now his muddy shoes betrayed him, For not an instant longer did Don doubt that the man could walk and run, and the crippled state was nothing but a ruse.

"No wonder he pumped me about who it was that sent the wigwag," he thought, as the sound of water was heard from the kitchen pump. "While I have been sitting here telling him everything he has been measuring me, wondering if I have been playing some sort of a game with him. Maybe I'm lucky that he didn't jump on me suddenly, but I believe that my straightforward story has convinced him that I don't know anything. Nothing dumb about him, evidently! My story about running down to see if he is all right must sound pretty flat, though."

The man wheeled into the room rapidly and in his hand he had a tall glass of water. Don drank it eagerly, keeping a wary eye on the old man, but nothing out of the way happened and he thanked him for the water.

"Don't mention it," smiled the man. "Come up again and see me, won't you?"

"I surely will," promised Don, as he opened the door. "Good night, sir."

"Good night, boy, good night," was the bright and cheery response, as Don went out.

"If he isn't a cripple, he certainly knows how to run that chair of his," Don decided, as he ran up the hill.

He found that the others were waiting for him impatiently. "Golly, we thought that you were lost," sad Jordan, impatiently.

"No, just talking with Mr. Vancouver," said Don. "Didn't have any luck, eh?"

"Not a bit," returned the senior captan. "Well, I suppose we may as well head in."

It did not take them long to make camp, where they found the others awaiting them. Jordan reported to the colonel, who had heard the shot and who knew from Rowen's own report what had happened. Howes was ordered to blow the bugle as a sign of recall, and before very long all of the groups had returned.

"Too bad we lost him," said the colonel, shaking his head. "I believe it was entirely due to Mr. Rowen's disobedience. I have ordered him into permanent arrest, until I decide what to do with him. Sound taps, Mr. Howes."

Don thought deeply before falling asleep. "I guess I'll keep things to myself, at least for a time," he decided. "It all sounds so farfetched that I hate to drag out my discoveries. But that man was surely out of his chair and out of his house this night! Now that I have something definite to work on something tangible may come up before long. The next thing we had better do is to find out who that mysterious flagman was."

# CHAPTER 16

## LISTENING IN

THE following day the camp was vibrant with excitement as the cadets relived the events of the night before. Everyone, of course, lamented the fact that Rowen had unwisely frightened the ghost away, but the boys realized that there was nothing to do but wait for the ghost to walk again.

During the afternoon some of the cadets noticed a stranger enter the colonel's tent. The caller stayed a short time and then left, taking the road which led to Rideway. Later Jordan, Don and Jim were ordered to the colonel's tent. Having seen the visitor, they wondered if their summons was in any way connected with him.

"Come in, come in," invited the colonel as the boys approached his quarters. "I have a job for you to do, that is, if you are willing."

"Anything you say, Colonel," Don replied, speaking for the group.

"Perhaps you noticed that I had a visitor this afternoon." He looked at the three cadets before him expectantly and they nodded to affirm this. "That was Mr. Farnsworth, the superintendent of the local telephone exchange in Rideway. It seems that his night operator was suddenly taken ill this morning and will be unable to go on duty tonight. He has no extra help at this time and thought perhaps one of the cadets knew how to operate a switchboard."

"I have run our switchboard at school a few times," said Jim, hesitantly. "However, I imagine this one in Rideway is far more complicated."

"Splendid!" said the colonel. "I thought I remembered correctly that you had, Jim. You will have no trouble at all with this local exchange. Mr. Farnsworth assured me that it was a simple board, else he would not have approached me. You see, this exchange is a small one and does not require a complicated system such as those one finds in large cities."

"Well, I'll do my best, sir," promised Jim. "I'm sure of that. Now, Don and Jordan, I want you to accompany Jim. You are to be at the exchange from midnight until seven o'clock, so perhaps three of you can keep one another awake for that period. Mr. Farnsworth will meet you there and show you what to do. Now, I suggest that you try to get some sleep before midnight. You will be awakened at the proper time and when you get to Rideway go to the building on the left of the town hall.

"You never can tell," the colonel continued with a wink, "but what this job may be far from dull. Remember that you are still members of the Ghost Patrol. Be alert!"

The three lucky cadets went immediately to their tents to talk over the piece of good news. They ate supper and after an hour turned in to sleep. Terry wailed at the fate that had left him out of it.

"Some guys have all the luck," he whined in a voice imitating Dick Rowen's. "I can't stand these Mercer boys, anyway. Besides, I've got the biggest ears and the colonel should have sent me."

The Officer of the Guard awakened the boys at the proper hour and they left the camp, passing the sentries safely. It did not take them long to cross the Ridge and strike down into Rideway. They found the streets totally deserted. Alongside the town hall they found the proper building and at their knock they were admitted by Mr. Farnsworth. He wore a telephone headset, consisting of one phone, a curved mouthpiece that fastened to the soundbox which rested on his chest, and a long, detachable plug.

He showed them the switchboard bearing scores of small white buttons that lighted up when the calls came in, and rows of multiple holes into which the plugs were inserted when calls were connected. He explained things in brief detail to them.

"This is what they call a manual board, as against a dial board," he said. "We have five girls working here in the daytime, but one operator is sufficient at night. Now, unless you have some questions, I'll be leaving."

"I think I understand this sort of system," answered Jim promptly. "It shouldn't cause us any trouble."

Thus assured, Mr. Farnsworth left. Then the three boys got a fair insight into the night telephone operator's job. There was complete silence until two-thirty when a call was received. Jim handled it expertly. There were few calls after that and the time went by much too slowly for the three active boys.

"This certainly is a lonely job," remarked Jordan, around a quarter after three.

"Yes, but I imagine you get used to it after a while," answered Don.

Just at that moment the switchboard buzzed twice. "Hmm, long distance," murmured Jim. "Mr. Farnsworth mentioned that two short rings was the signal for a long-distance call."

He plugged in below the lighted signal. At his answer a dull voice said, "Let me have Main 7200."

Jordan was about to speak when Jim sat bolt upright and signaled to the others to be silent. His eyes grew as big as saucers as he listened intently. Don and Jordan were mystified by his actions, but they said not a word. It seemed an interminable length of time before Jim closed the key and plugged into another line.

"What is it? What's the matter?" Don questioned his brother eagerly.

"I'll tell you all about it in a minute. I've got to do something first!"

The others listened impatiently while Jim held a short conversation with someone who seemed to be another operator. At last Jim removed the headset and turned to his companions.

"That was a call to the drugstore and it was about the ghost!" Jim said breathlessly.

"What!" exclaimed Don and Jordan together. "I was just on the point of closing the key, after making sure that the connection was correct, when I heard someone say, 'Those cadets chased the ghost into the old Furmen house and very nearly caught him.' That's when I motioned to you not to talk. Then the other voice said, 'Those meddling cadets again, was it?' and the person at the drugstore, who gave his name as Rose, answered, 'Yes, Mr. Maul.'"

"Maul!" shouted Don. "Why, that's the name of the family the Hydes had a feud with!"

"Then there is one of them still alive," Jordan said thoughtfully.

"That's the same conclusion I reached," Jim said. "I just checked the origin of the call with the operator and she told me it was from a pay station in Crossland."

"Golly! Wait until the colonel hears about this. I'll bet he never dreamed we would really come up with something tonight," Jordan said excitedly.

"But I haven't told you everything," Jim interrupted. "The man named Maul gave the clerk instructions to relay to the ghost. He is to go to him this afternoon and tell him to start prowling on the far side of the Ridge. In about a week he said he would send orders referring to another attempt to burn the Hydes out. His final word was, 'First I will get rid of those schoolboy soldiers.'"

"That means another chance to catch the ghost!" exclaimed Jordan. "Say, we ought to trail that clerk when he goes out this afternoon."

"And I'll tell you just where he will go, too," said Don calmly. He had been unusually quiet during the conversation between his brother and Jordan, because he had been thinking things out.

"Where?" the others demanded.

"To the cabin of Peter Vancouver," returned Don.

"Why to him?" asked Jordan. "He's lame and can't get about."

"My best uniform that he isn't," Don laughed. "Let me tell you what happened the night we chased the ghost." With that he related the story of his visit to Vancouver's cabin. "I'm positive that he had been out that night, and I don't think for a minute that he is an invalid at all."

"Without arousing suspicion, let's try to find out from Mr. Farnsworth how long the man has been living in that cabin," Jim suggested.

The others agreed to the idea and waited impatiently for seven o'clock to come. At last it did and Mr. Farnsworth was prompt.

He thanked them earnestly and inquired whether they had had any difficulties. Jim assured him he had not. Mr. Farnsworth was a friendly person and was very interested in the cadets' activities. He kept the boys there for a few minutes, asking them questions concerning their camp life.

The superintendent's interest enabled the boys to describe their hikes through the countryside and, in passing, Jim told him of their visit to Peter Vancouver. He then casually asked Mr. Farnsworth if Vancouver was a native of the region.

"Oh, no," was the man's reply. "He moved here only a few years ago. No one knows much about him. He keeps to himself, though of course that's natural since he's confined to a wheelchair."

After a few minutes of further conversation the cadets departed.

They struck the trail for camp at a rapid pace.

"Good golly, I am hungry," sighed Jim, as they topped the rise.

"I guess we all are," replied Jordan. "But we have made splendid progress in the last few hours. What a rare piece of luck that you listened in on that call, Jim!"

They arrived in camp while drill was going on and reported at once to the colonel. He was interested and pleased beyond measure.

"That is splendid work, boys," he approved, heartily. "Now, some of you must do some active trailing. I suppose you three feel equal to the observation task, don't you?"

"We will after we have had some breakfast, sir," Don smiled back.

"Of course. Report to the mess tent at once. Pack something up to take with you and then get your field glasses and find a post from which you can watch the cabin of this supposed cripple. I compliment you on your fine powers of observation regarding this Peter Vancouver, Don."

"Thank you, sir," acknowledged Don. "It is a clever game all the way through, and only lucky accidents have put us in touch with the truth."

"Yes, the kind of accidents that you boys always seem to have," said the colonel, dryly. "Well, run along to your breakfast."

"We're having all the fun," grinned Jim, as they hiked once more to the top of the Ridge a short time later. "Won't old redhead pull his hair out in handfuls when he hears of this!"

A small clump of bushes on a high hill gave them a good view of Vancouver's cabin when sighted through the glasses and there was no danger that they would be seen in turn. The morning passed without any sign of anything moving and they ate their lunch under a hot sun.

"He surely ought to show up this afternoon," Jordan thought.

"If he waits until nightfall we're licked," said Jim.

The afternoon dragged until four o'clock, and then Jordan uttered an exclamation. He had his glasses pointed at the cabin.

"Here he comes now," he announced, and the others raised their glasses. Sure enough, a man was wending his way up the slope, straight for Vancouver's cabin, and Jim called their attention to a white package that he had in his hand.

The clerk stayed in the cabin for an hour and departed at the end of that time. When he had gone, Jordan closed his glass.

"That makes the case complete," he announced. "Now we can go back and report to the colonel. Who wants to bet that I don't stay up until taps tonight?"

"Not I," returned Jim, promptly, "I'm so dead on my feet right now that I won't know whether you do or not!"

# CHAPTER 17

## BREAKING UP HYDES' PARTY

On the following morning Colonel Morrell had an early and unexpected visitor. He was a fairly good-looking young man, with a handsome smile and a confident air. Without introducing himself he asked the colonel of the cadet corps an astonishing question.

"Well, what luck did you have with the ghost the other night?" the man inquired with a pleasant smile.

There was a pause before the colonel answered him. "Unfortunately we missed him after a considerable chase. Are you the one who—?"

"Yes, I sent you the wigwag," replied the young man. "I am a scoutmaster over in Rideway and that's how I happen to know the signals. I've been wanting to put this stupid ghost out of business and saw this opportunity to do it."

"How did you come to find out that the ghost was going to walk, Mr.—?" began the colonel.

"My name is Benson," explained the other. "Between 1:00 a.m. and 8:00 a.m. I am employed as a telephone operator on the local switchboard. I was suddenly taken ill the other day or I would have been up to see you sooner."

"Oh, so you're the night operator. Some of our boys filled in for you in your absence."

"Mr. Farnsworth has told me about that. It was very kind of you, sir."

"It is good training for our boys. It makes them realize their responsibility as citizens to help in any sort of emergency which may arise, I believe. But tell me why you warned us of the ghost's activities."

"It was really an accident that I heard a conversation that morning which gave me the information. There was a long-distance telephone call made to our local drugstore. I connected the line and rang. Then, forgetting to close my key more than anything else, I listened while the receiver was picked up at the drugstore. I was pretty sleepy at the time, but I was knocked wide awake by hearing the party on the far end of the wire say: 'What are the latest activities, Rose? I know about the failure to burn Hyde's farm. Has the ghost walked since?' That staggered me and I listened closely to what followed."

Colonel Morrell leaned forward in his chair. The story of the young scout leader was of great interest to him.

Mr. Benson continued. "The voice at the other end was a low, cold sort of voice, and I was trying to catch a clue from it, hoping that the clerk would use a name, but he didn't. He just kept using the title Sir. This voice at the other end said: 'I know all about those cadets interfering with the activities of the ghost, and I will attend to them personally very soon. When I do, they won't have so much as a tent left to them or a single horse! But I don't want the ghost to stay in just because of those soldiers. Tell him to get moving again, and make it his business not to get caught.' It was that last statement which caused me to get word to you."

"And a good thing it was, too," replied Colonel Morrell. He then proceeded to tell Mr. Benson the facts that the boys had uncovered. When he had finished he said, "Rest assured that we will get to the bottom of this unpleasant business. I will keep you informed of any further developments, As soon as he left, Colonel Morrell called the Mercers and Jordan together for a conference.

"It seems you are not the only person guilty of listening in on telephone conversations, Jim," he began. Then he told them of Mr. Benson's visit. "Now I think the next step is to engage a good private detective and see if we can't have this man Maul located in Crossland. If we merely arrest the paid ghost and don't get the big man higher up we will accomplish nothing."

At the evening meal in the mess tent the colonel addressed his corps.

"Boys, some time ago we pledged ourselves to run down this ghost business that is troubling the inhabitants of the Ridge and to date we have made quite a bit of progress, even more than most of you know. In due time full details will be related to you, but at present it seems best to keep things quiet. But this much I wish to tell you: we have learned that this 'ghost' is a hired professional who is planning to wipe out our camp. I do not know just how he proposes to do it, whether by fire or mob violence, but it is planned, and according to the information secured the blow will come soon. I am therefore doubling the number of sentries beginning with tonight. Your orders are to alarm the camp instantly if anything out of the ordinary is seen or heard. The Officers of the Guard will exercise unwavering care and conduct rigid inspection of posts."

The colonel resumed his seat and there was a buzz of excitement and indignation. The cadets welcomed the prospect for some actual and dangerous service, and the prospect of a mob fight was especially alluring. But the feeling was that any move made against them would be in the nature of a stealthy act, and all of the cadets determined to brace themselves for the stern business at hand.

"If any ghost tries to touch the horses I'll shoot him on sight," growled Thompson, who loved the animals.

"All I hope is that they rush the camp with a gang," Terry said. "Wouldn't that be a swell scrap! Imagine the corps meeting a crowd of roughnecks in a hand-to-hand battle. That would be something to write about!"

"If you were able to write, Redhead," said a cadet near by.

"Gee, if the battalion couldn't lick any bunch recruited around here we ought to go back to the school and play tennis all the rest of our lives," snorted Terry, who was not good at the sport and therefore did not like it.

"I'm afraid that the attack won't be an open one," Don told them. "More likely to be something shady."

"You ought to know, Mercer," said Motley. "Wish I had been on that switchboard the other night."

That night the number of guards was doubled and the greatest care was exercised. The Officers of the Guard visited posts at frequent intervals and checked up on the sentries. But the night went by without anything out of the ordinary happening. In the morning Benson brought news.

"That ghost showed up in South Plains last night," he reported. "Some farmers saw him over that way. That is some distance from here and the ghost is following orders to the letter. I didn't hear a thing last night, though I listened to every conversation. Tonight he may come back this way. But I don't know whether you will have to fear him or not, for if you'll remember Maul promised to do the job himself."

"We'll be on the lookout for both of them," promised the colonel.

That afternoon was a warm one and the boys went swimming. Terry had developed a slight summer cold and so he did not go. He was sitting in front of the tent on a box whittling a piece of wood industriously. The camp was quiet and the shouts of the cadets in the swimming hole drifted to his ears.

There was a voice near Terry and he looked up. The little Carson boy was approaching down the company street from the direction of the woods and Terry waved to him.

"Hi, Jimmie," greeted Terry. "How are you today?"

"OK, Terry," smiled the boy. "Why aren't you in swimming?"

"Got a little cold and the company doctor told me to stay out for a while," answered the whittler, gravely. "What's on your mind today, anything in particular?"

"I want to tell you something," said Jimmie Carson, sitting down on the edge of the box as Terry made room for him. "You know that old man over in the cabin? The man named Vancouver?"

"Yes, I know who he is. Why?"

"Well, what do you think, Mr. Mackson? He isn't lame at all!"

Terry stopped his whittling abruptly and looked keenly at Jimmie. "How do you know that?" he demanded.

"I heard the Hydes say so," was the reply. "They are going over there tonight and kill him or something!"

The whittling ceased for good.

"The Hydes!" cried Terry. "How did they know?"

"Listen, I was over at the Hydes with my father this morning," said the boy, his eyes serious and grave. "While Pop was talking to old man Hyde I heard the sons talking in the barn. They didn't know that I was right outside on our wagon, and I heard them plainly. They said that one of them had seen the man sneak into his cabin late last night, and they found out that he wasn't any cripple. Seems that one of the Hydes was driving home from some place and he saw the ghost sneak into the cabin. Then he looked in under a window and saw the ghost get back into his chair, so they knew that old man was playing ghost. Can you imagine that, Mr. Mackson?"

"No, I can't," returned Terry gravely.

"So they said they was going to go to the cabin tonight and just about kill that old man. I thought at first I'd tell Pa, but I was scared to, so I come up here to tell you fellows about it. I don't think that old man ought to be hit by those big bully Hydes, do you?"

"No, sir," said Terry, with emphasis. "Jimmie boy, I'm glad you told me this. Come along to the colonel; we must tell him."

The colonel was keenly interested in the news. "Thank you for telling us this, my boy," he smiled down at the rugged lad. "This old man is a wicked fellow to go around scaring people out of their wits, but just as you say he shouldn't be hit by those Hydes. Mr. Mackson, pass the word to the special patrol to be ready to go with me to the cabin as soon as darkness comes tonight."

"Very well, Colonel," said Terry. "I'm glad you are going along, because I feel that this is likely to be a fairly tough situation."

They left the tent and Terry went to hunt up the other boys, first swearing little Jimmie to secrecy. "Don't breath a word of it," he told the boy. "We want to save this old man from a severe beating and we also want to capture him for his part in the business that has been going on around here. So it will be the best thing if you keep very quiet about it."

"I will, Terry," promised the lad.

The others soon knew what was expected of them. Just before they started out they met in the tent of the colonel.

"Mr. Vench and Mr. Douglas, I want you to start right away for Rideway and get the sheriff," ordered the colonel. "We can't arrest this man ourselves, but he must do it. It may be that we shall have trouble with the Hydes, and anyway, the sheriff is always saying that we interfere with his affairs on the Ridge. You may have trouble with the sheriff, but if you do just tell him that your colonel requests him to come to the cabin."

"Very well, sir," Douglas responded, and he and Vench went out.

"We will take side arms with us," said the colonel, buckling on a revolver belt. "We won't have to use them, I trust, but at least we'll be prepared." When the others of the Ghost Patrol had equipped themselves they set out with the colonel for the cabin over the hill. Those in the camp saw them go and much speculation went around as to the purpose of the expedition. The camp itself was in order for any emergency, with double guards posted and the major in charge.

Vench and Douglas had obtained a good start and they felt it would not be long before they returned with the sheriff, if he could be persuaded to come. The others swung on toward the little cabin at a rapid pace, topping the rise and bearing down on it.

"Somebody's at home," Don said, as they came in sight. "There are lights in the windows."

"Yes, but look! There are the Hydes!" said Terry, pointing.

Into the patch of light from one of the small windows a burly figure stepped and another joined it. A third figure proclaimed the father. There was a word of planning between them and then one of the sons raised his foot and kicked the window deliberately out. With that action he jumped right through the opening and landed in the room. A moment of silence followed and then the front door was opened. Promptly the father and the other son walked in and the door was shut.

"Just in time," proclaimed the colonel, grimly. "Let us hustle, boys."

They ran down the rest of the slope, the doughty colonel in front, and came to the cabin in a short time. The colonel threw himself against the door, which had not been very well secured, and it opened under his impact. Followed by Don, Terry, Jim and Jordan, the colonel shot into the room.

In one corner crouched the supposed invalid, his face pale and his hands grasping a stout stick. Facing him, with brutal expressions on their surly faces, stood the Hydes. The oldest son held a heavy horsewhip in his hands, and it was evident that he was just going to use it when the cadet party burst in.

At sight of the cadets the expressions on their faces changed. Surprise gave way to eager gladness on the face of the old man and spiteful anger on the faces of the Hydes. As yet no blow had fallen and the relief party was in the nick of time.

"What do you want here?" the father said, a snarl in his voice.

"We want that man, for playing the part of a ghost and stampeding our horses," said the colonel evenly. "And we want to see to it that you don't touch that man with your whip."

"You do, eh?" grunted the son with the whip. "You all can have this old man if you want him, but you can't stop us from whipping the daylights out of him. This is the dog that burned our barn down."

"I know all about that," nodded the colonel. "But you won't horsewhip him. You can turn him over to the proper authorities; in fact, I have already sent for the sheriff and he will be here any minute now. But you can't take the law into your own hands, not while we are here, certainly."

"Look here, you soldier captain, or whatever you are!" bellowed the senior Hyde. "You mind your own business. Putting this fellow in jail won't do us any good, and we're going to beat the hide off him. You keep out. Josh, go ahead and wallop him."

The Hyde boy raised his whip but the colonel reached up, jerked it from his hand and threw it into a far corner. The Hydes grew red and clenched their fists.

"Let's give them a good beating, Pa," said the younger son, and he advanced. But the colonel drew his revolver and covered the three of them. The other cadets dropped their hands to the butts of their guns.

"Come a step nearer me and I'll shoot you right through the leg," promised the colonel, simply.

The threat stopped them in their tracks. Sullenly they fell back, hatred showing in their faces. The old man whooped faintly.

"That's handling them," he said, stirring eagerly. The colonel looked at him.

"You stay where you are, too, Mr. Vancouver," he said. "We'll have to turn you over to the law for punishment."

"I ain't the only one in this game," blustered the old man.

"We know all about Mr. Maul," said the colonel. The Hydes snapped to attention.

"Maul!" cried the father, harshly. "Old Maul is dead!"

"Old Maul is very much alive," retorted the colonel. "He is the one who is directing this whole campaign. Did you think this old man was doing it for fun? He has been paid by Maul to keep this thing going, and he planned to burn you out of your house pretty shortly."

"Then you ought to let us whip this sneaking skunk!" shouted the elder Hyde.

"Brutality won't do any good," returned the headmaster.

"Here comes the sheriff," announced Jordan, as a heavy step was heard outside the door.

The door opened to admit the sheriff, followed by Vench and Douglas. The two cadets looked grave and a trifle angry and the sheriff was his usual blustering self.

"What's going on here?" he roared, looking around. His angry eyes fastened themselves on the colonel. "I hear that you requested me to come up here. Requested me! Who are you, sir? I never saw you in my life!"

"I never saw you either," said the unmoved colonel.

"What is the trouble here, anyway?" demanded the sheriff.

The trouble was explained by the colonel, but the sheriff shrugged his shoulders. "I think you would have done well to have minded your own business, sir," said the officious man. "This man needs a sound horsewhipping. If it had been your house he burned you would be the first one to whip him. What am I supposed to do?"

"You will arrest the old man and put him where he will be safe," said the colonel. "As for the Hydes, you can't do anything but send them home."

"Look here, colonel, are you giving me orders!" bellowed the loud sheriff, his face a dull red. "If you are, I won't even listen to them. Where you get the nerve to order me around is more than I can see. I've got half a mind to run you in for pointing a revolver at the Hydes."

"Sheriff," said the colonel, hotly. "I'll tell you what I'm going to do with you. I'm going to let the world know how a ghost terrorized the Ridge here for years, right under your nose, and you never found out who it was. I'm going to relate how my boys discovered the whole thing, and if you ever get another job with responsibility to it, I don't know what the people of this county are thinking of!"

There was a total silence in the room while the colonel and the sheriff glared at each other. The whole frame of the sheriff shook with suppressed rage and his breath came fast. Calmly the colonel looked him straight in the eye. But the sheriff was beaten and he knew it.

Instead he vented his fury upon the Hydes. "Get out of here and get home," he snarled. "Don't ever let me catch you in any trouble again as long as I'm sheriff on this Ridge! You, Peter Vancouver, come here while I put the handcuffs on you."

# CHAPTER 18

## THE LAST OF THE GHOST

The Hydes had slunk off and were lost in the darkness. The sheriff had handcuffed Peter Vancouver and now they were on their way to the local jail in Rideway. After putting the light out the colonel and the members of the Ghost Patrol left the cabin and started over the trail to camp.

"I'm very glad we got there in time to prevent any serious injury to that old man," remarked the colonel, as they walked on. "Did you boys have any trouble with that sheriff?"

"A little bit, sir," Douglas replied. "He made a lot of noise when we explained things to him. But he did come finally, though he talked so much and made so much noise on the way up that Vench and I felt like rolling him in the mud!"

"I guess it was about time that somebody talked to him," the colonel said. "The people around here are curious. They haven't made any effort to run down this ghost and they take abuse from this great blustering sheriff. But I guess this ghost angle of things is about over."

"All that remains now is to catch Maul," Jordan reminded him.

"Yes, and we'll see to it that steps are taken to do that," the headmaster promised.

The sky was pitch black, and not a star in sight. A leaden sky threatened rain and the absence of the moon and the friendly stars made the world below very dark indeed. Fortunately for them the cadets knew the road fairly well, and they approached the camp through the bushes without having altered their course enough to puzzle them.

"We will be hailed in about a moment," said the colonel. They were close to the outpost where the sentry was on duty, and they advanced boldly, waiting for the call.

But none came. They reached the line of patrol that the sentry was supposed to make, but they did not run across the man who should have been patrolling. In bewilderment they stopped.

"This is very queer," murmured the colonel. "What can have happened?"

Terry moved forward and struck his foot against something soft. Without loss of time he dropped to his knees, feeling before him with his hands. The sharp intake of his breath drew their attention.

"What is it?" the colonel asked, quickly.

"Here is the sentry, tied up tighter than a bundle," was the startling reply. "Something's fishy around here."

The others clustered around and a match was struck. They found Cadet Innes, the sentry, lying on his back, bound around with coarse but strong cord. He seemed to be all right otherwise, but perfectly speechless with a thick gag in his mouth. By the way his eyes snapped they judged that he had plenty to say. When the grunts of surprise were over they went to work and soon relieved him of the ropes and the gag.

"Be quiet, on your lives, men!" was his first word, after he had licked his dry lips. "The man who tied me up is in the camp, up to something."

"Any idea who it was, Mr. Innes?" the colonel whispered.

"No, sir. A man all in black jumped me and did it in a hurry. Muzzled me with one hand and took away my gun with the other. It happened before the Officer of the Guard got around, in fact he is due here now."

"You say the man went toward the camp?" was the colonel's next question.

"Yes, sir, and he carried a can of kerosene with him," was the startling reply. The others wasted not another minute, but jumped to their feet.

"Be very quiet as you approach the camp," ordered the colonel, leading the way through the bushes toward the camp.

They approached silently and looked at the camp. It seemed deserted. Three fires showed up red before the tents, but the cadets were in their beds. On the other side of the camp the Officers of the Guard could be heard as he spoke shortly to a sentry. Otherwise there seemed to be no movement or life in the place.

Don reached over and pulled the colonel's arm. Close to the supply wagons a darker shadow showed, and the faint sound of liquid bubbling out of a can could be heard. All of the hidden watchers caught the significance of it at once and crouched down to wait until the man should have come nearer them.

Then, something happened that changed their plans abruptly.

A match was struck. The flare of the tiny blaze showed a set, stern face. The man at the supply wagon bent forward with the match.

Cadet Vench was little. He was also fast and happened to be the nearest one to the stooping man. In three strides Vench left the shelter of the trees, sprang into the air, and landed like a monkey on the back of the man, who had started to straighten up at the sound of Vench's steps. They both went down, the match dropped on some oil-soaked cloth, and a fierce blaze jumped up in a twinkling.

As Jim afterward said, he staked all on the size of his feet. He landed with both shoes on the cloth, snuffed the blaze out with a single stroke, and saved the supply wagons and the entire camp.

Now all was action. A sentry near by had fired the alarm. Vench and the unknown man were staging a furious wrestling match on the ground beside the wagons as the others dashed up and came to his help. Someone threw more fuel on the nearest fire, Major Rhodes ran up with his revolver in hand, and the whole camp, more or less dressed, came running after him. In the new light which the fire showed they saw Vench and the colonel drag the man to his feet.

"Just got you in time," said the colonel, holding the man in a tight grip. "Am I right when I say your name is probably Maul?"

"Yes, my name is Jackson Maul," was the reply, given in a deep voice. He gazed in haughty silence around at the gaping cadets.

"I'll ask you to spend the rest of the night with us in our guard tent, Mr. Maul," said the colonel, his revolver in his hand. "I may as well tell you that your ghost game is up, and the ghost of the Ridge safe in the county jail. I think you'll find yourself in pretty heavy trouble for attempting to fire our camp."

No reply was offered by the man who called himself Maul and they took him away, where a tent could serve as his place of imprisonment. Major Rhodes himself took the responsibility of watching him for the rest of the night. It was some time before the excited cadets went back to their beds. An examination showed them that the camp had been soaked in oil at a number of points, and had fire been applied to any of these places they would have been totally wiped out. It would have been a lucky thing if they had all escaped with their lives had the camp been fired.

On the following morning the man Maul was marched to Rideway and locked in jail with the man he had paid to play ghost. The full story now spread around the town and the Ridge people found out how they had been terrorized for years by the last of the Maul family in his effort to drive the Hydes away. With this capture of the two men the mystery of the ghost of Rustling Ridge came to an end, and from that time forward the inhabitants had nothing more to fear after dark. In time the two men and the clerk Rose were all given prison terms for mischief with malicious intent. The Hydes kept out of trouble from that time forward and the loud sheriff of the Ridge became softer in his speech, at least as long as the cadets were in the neighborhood. A number of the county newspapers gave high praise to the cadets and to Benson, the night telephone operator, for public-spirited duty.

Soon after these events the colonel called Rowen into his tent. He had been very much displeased with the conduct of the cadet, but as he reflected that things had now settled down, it would be wise to forget the whole thing, he felt sure. So he spoke mildly enough to the cadet, but he was surprised when the sulky one flared back at him.

"Never mind, Colonel Morrell, I don't want to talk about anything!" was the astonishing statement. "I'm going home right away. Everything has been pushed against me during this whole encampment and I'm sick of it! I don't want anything more to do with the cadet corps!"

"Very well, Mr. Rowen," returned the colonel, still mildly. "You say everything has been pushed against you. But you would not believe Mercer's word about the ghost starting the stampede. Now we have the word of the ghost himself that he started it and that Jim called out to him. Then, against orders, you took your revolver with you and shot it off at an improper time. Under those circumstances, do you still feel that you had everything against you on this camping trip?"

"I feel that I have had enough of this school and this trip," said Rowen. "I guess I could have more fun with my own friends in a summer camp where a fellow didn't have to do so much unnecessary work. I'm going home."

Mr. Rowen did go home. No one was really sorry to see him go, for his surly temper had never made him popular in any way.

From that time onward the summer slipped along without unusual incident. It was a delightful and happy vacation, full of swinging action and invigorating fun, and when the time came to break camp all of the boys were a little bit sorry.

"Back to school again," said Don, as they struck tents.

"Yes, and our time is getting limited," said Terry, seriously. "We haven't a whole lot more time left to us in our school life."

"Right you are," Jim agreed. "Next year Don will be senior captain of the school."

Before the morning was over the cadet battalion was marching toward the school, leaving Rustling Ridge and its many exciting memories behind them.